I0584683

Happiness

Book by
John Weidman

Music by
Scott Frankel

Lyrics by
Michael Korie

Original Direction and
Choreography by
Susan Stroman

FOR PRODUCTION INQUIRIES

UNITED STATES AND CANADA
info@concordtheatricals.com
1-866-979-0447

UNITED KINGDOM AND EUROPE
licensing@concordtheatricals.co.uk
020-7054-7298

Each title is subject to availability from Concord Theatricals Corp., depending upon country of performance. Please be aware that *HAPPINESS* may not be licensed by Concord Theatricals Corp. in your territory. Professional and amateur producers should contact the nearest Concord Theatricals Corp. office or licensing partner to verify availability.

No one shall make any changes in this title(s) for the purpose of production. No part of this book may be reproduced, stored in a retrieval system, scanned, uploaded, or transmitted in any form, by any means, now known or yet to be invented, including mechanical, electronic, digital, photocopying, recording, videotaping, or otherwise, without the prior written permission of the publisher. No one shall share this title(s), or any part of this title(s), through any social media or file hosting websites.

For all inquiries regarding motion picture, television, online/digital and other media rights, please contact Concord Theatricals Corp.

THIRD-PARTY MATERIALS USE NOTE

Licensees are solely responsible for obtaining formal written permission from copyright owners to use copyrighted third-party materials (e.g., incidental music not provided in connection with a performance license, artworks, logos) in the performance of this play and are strongly cautioned to do so. If no such permission is obtained by the licensee, then the licensee must use only original materials and materials that the licensee owns and controls. Licensees are solely responsible and liable for clearances of all third-party copyrighted materials, and shall indemnify the copyright owners of the play(s) and their licensing agent, Concord Theatricals Corp., against any costs, expenses, losses and liabilities arising from the use of such copyrighted third-party materials by licensees. For music, please contact the appropriate music licensing authority in your territory for the rights to any incidental music not provided in connection with a performance license.

IMPORTANT BILLING AND CREDIT REQUIREMENTS

If you have obtained performance rights to this title, please refer to your licensing agreement for important billing and credit requirements.

HAPPINESS was first produced by the Lincoln Center Theater in New York City on February 27th, 2009. The performance was directed and choreographed by Susan Stroman and assistant directed and choreographed by Joanne Manning, with sets by Thomas Lynch, costumes by William Ivey Long, lighting design by Donald Holder, sound by Scott Lehrer, orchestrations by Bruce Coughlin, music direction by Eric Stern, and projection design by Joshua Frankel. The Production Stage Manager was Rolt Smith. The cast was as follows:

ZACK	Sebastian Arcelus
MIGUEL	Miguel Cervantes
GINA	Jenny Powers
HELEN	Phyllis Somerville
CINDY	Pearl Sun
NEIL	Robert Petkoff
KEVIN	Fred Applegate
MAURICE	Ken Page
ARLENE	Joanna Gleason
STANLEY	Hunter Foster
HYACINTH	Idara Victor
YOUNG HELEN/ENSEMBLE	Alessa Neeck
TOMMY/ALBERT/JASON	Patrick Cummings
YOUNG KEVIN	Alexander Sheitinger
KEVIN'S DAD/LUTHER	James Moye
JUANITA	Ana Maria Andricain
YOLANDA	Lina Silver
MICK/MARCELLO	Robb Sapp
ENSEMBLE	Holly Ann Butler, Janet Dickinson, Alan H. Green, Samantha Maza, Eric Santagata, Matt Wall

CHARACTERS

ZACK – a workaholic lawyer struggling to make partner at his firm, early thirties

MIGUEL – a bicycle delivery messenger, early twenties, divorced

GINA – a perfume counter salesperson with an active imagination, late thirties

HELEN – a widow in the beginning stages of senescence, seventies

CINDY – a soon-to-be-doctor in residence at a New York hospital

NEIL – Cindy's husband, also a resident physician

KEVIN – a middle-aged Park Avenue doorman

MAURICE – a well-connected society interior decorator

ARLENE – a politically conservative talk radio host

STANLEY – an MTA subway train conductor

OTHERS

HYACINTH – a homecare and hospital nurse

YOUNG HELEN – Helen's younger homefront self during World War II

TOMMY – a young Army serviceman about to be shipped off to Anzio

YOUNG KEVIN – Kevin back when he was a baseball-loving kid

KEVIN'S DAD – a working class father, a doorman like Kevin will become

LUTHER – lead singer of Spooky Tooth at the Fillmore East

JUANITA – Miguel's ex-wife

YOLANDA – Miguel's young daughter

MICK – a celebrated English rock star

MARCELLO – a recent immigrant from Italy, Gina's one-time boyfriend

ENSEMBLE plays additional characters including a **CABBIE**; **SMOOTHIE SALESPERSON**; **USO SINGERS & DANCERS**; **RUSS HODGES**, a radio sports commentator; **WILLIE MAYS**; **AIRLINE PASSENGERS & PERSONNEL**; **SUITED BUSINESSMEN**; **YOLANDA'S FRIEND**; **ROCK CLUB DANCERS**; and a **YOUNG WOMAN** (on the subway platform).

SETTING
New York City.

TIME
2008.

SONGS

1. Just Not Right Now . . . . Zack & Company
2. Blips . . . . Stanley
3. Flibberty Jibbers And Wobbly Knees . . . . Helen, USO Vocalists, Young Helen, Tommy
4. Best Seats In The Ballpark . . . . Kevin, Young Kevin, Kevin's Father, Company
5. Gstaad . . . . Gina & Company
6. The Boy Inside Your Eyes . . . . Maurice & Albert
7. Perfect Moments . . . . Company
8. Step Up The Ladder . . . . Stanley & Company
9. Just Not Right Now – Reprise . . . . Zack
10. Family Flashcards . . . . Neil & Cindy
11. The Tooth Fairy Song . . . . Miguel & Yolanda
12. Road To Nirvana . . . . Arlene & Company
13. Gstaad – Reprise . . . . Gina & Marcello
14. Happiness . . . . Zack & Stanley
15. Blips – Reprise . . . . Stanley

Happiness is performed without an intermission.

Zack's Apartment, The Upper West Side

(Downstage, a small kitchen island. On it, an automatic coffee maker, laptop, bottle of vitamins, and a box of Power Bars, flipped open. Snap! The coffee maker burbles on. Lights out...)

[MUSIC NO. 1 "OVERTURE"]

(A musical fanfare plays and then a clock radio erupts. Lights up on...)

[MUSIC NO. 2 "JUST NOT RIGHT NOW"]

*(**ZACK**, an intense associate at an elite New York law firm. He appears upstage, wearing a robe and reading e-mail on his BlackBerry. Then he makes his way downstage and pours himself a cup of coffee.)*

ZACK.
THIS IS MY MAKE OR BREAK MORNING.
THIS IS MY NAME ON THE DOOR.
THIS IS THE DAY MY SUMMATION
NAILS THE PLAINTIFF TO THE FLOOR.
TIME FOR THIS BOY TO MAKE PARTNER,
EVEN IN TIMES LIKE TODAY.
SHOW 'EM MY SMARTS AND ENDURANCE,
AS MY SMILE OF SELF-ASSURANCE SEEMS TO SAY...
...IT'S JUST ANOTHER NEW YORK MONDAY.
ANOTHER MILLION DOLLAR WIN.
ANOTHER HOSTILE JUDGE AND JURY
I BE-DAZZLE WITH A GRIN.

ZACK.
> ANOTHER NOSEDIVE FOR THE NASDAQ.
> ANOTHER DOWNTURN FOR THE DOW.
> MAYBE SOMEDAY I'LL WORK
> ON A RACQUETBALL SERVE THAT'LL WOW...

> *(He pops a vitamin into his mouth and grabs his coffee.)*

> JUST NOT RIGHT NOW.

> *(He picks up a Power Bar, takes his coffee and his BlackBerry, and exits as...)*

> *(...A* **CROWD OF NEW YORKERS** *rushing off to work enters, wiping the stage and revealing...)*

A Sidewalk Outside Shorty's in Washington Heights

*(**MIGUEL**, a Hispanic bicycle messenger in his early thirties is riding his bicycle through the crowd. He has a messenger bag slung across his shoulder; the bag seems to be moving slightly. He dismounts and pulls out his cell phone.)*

MIGUEL. *(Talking on his phone.)* Yo, Uncle Manny. It's Miguel. Listen, I got your chicken – oh, sorry, your "Mayaguez Fighting Cock." But Manny, I'm a professional bicycle messenger, all right? Riding barnyard animals up and down the Bronx is not my thing. First time, last time, got it?

(He hangs up. The messenger bag clucks and shakes.)

SHUT UP, YOU BLOOD-THIRSTY CHICKEN.
NOBODY GETS A FREE RIDE.
BETTER BEHAVE OR YOUR SCRAWNY ASS
'LL BE KENTUCKY FRIED.

(His cell phone rings. He looks at the caller ID, grimaces, answers.)

What now, Juanita?

*(Another **CROWD OF NEW YORKERS** wipes the stage, revealing...)*

A Construction Site, Rego Park

(**GINA** *is standing on the corner talking on her cell phone. She is somewhere in her late thirties, stylishly attractive, dressed, and groomed – like the kind of saleswomen who work behind the cosmetics counters at Bloomingdale's.*)

(*Two* **HARD HATS** *stand behind her, drinking coffee, and admiring her ass.*)

HARD HAT #1. Damn, girl!

HARD HAT #2. Hey, baby!

GINA.
I UNDERSTAND SHE'S MY COUSIN.
R.S.V.P. MY REGRET.
THAT'S WHEN I'M FLYING TO CORFU
WITH SEBASTIAN ON HIS PRIVATE CHARTER JET.

Ma, I'm just saying her wedding is the same weekend I'm going to Greece.

MIGUEL. (*Impatiently, into phone.*) I know I'm behind with the alimony, Juanita. I'm pedaling as fast as I can.

GINA. Yes, with Sebastian... Ma, just because you never met him, doesn't –

HARD HAT #1. Hey, baby, my pal Vinnie wants to get in your pants!

GINA. (*Covering the phone.*) Tell your pal Vinnie one asshole in my pants is enough.

(*The* **HARD HATS** *hoot;* **GINA**, *back into phone, alternating with* **MIGUEL**, *unable to get a word in edgewise.*)

MIGUEL.
IT'S JUST ANOTHER NEW YORK MONDAY.
ANOTHER GO-ROUND WITH THE "EX."

GINA.
> I'M GONNA LOSE YOU, MA,
> I'M ON A TRAIN TO FIFTY-NINTH AND LEX.

MIGUEL.
> YOU'RE GONNA HAVE THE CHECK BY TUESDAY.

GINA.
> I'M HANGIN' UP THE PHONE SO "CIAO."

BOTH.
> LOOK, I HATE TO REFUSE YOU
> OUR USUAL SEVENTEEN ROUNDS.
> JUST NOT RIGHT NOW.

> *(**GINA** snaps the phone closed...)*

> *(...As simultaneously, **MIGUEL** snaps his cell phone closed and the messenger bag, which he has dropped on the sidewalk, shoots across the street.)*

MIGUEL. Oh, shit –

> *(He takes off after it, leaving his bike behind, as more **NEW YORKERS** enter, bustling across the stage.)*

> *(**ZACK**, suited up and carrying an expensive briefcase, works his way through the **CROWD** like a salmon swimming upstream.)*

ZACK.
> RIGHT NOW,
> WITH PANIC IN THE AIR,
> I NEED TO STAY THE COURSE
> TO GET MY RIGHTFUL SHARE.
> PRESTIGE AND SUCCESS,
> IN EQUAL AMOUNTS...

ZACK.
> THEN AFTER I'VE EARNED ENOUGH
> TO BE FREE FROM STRESS,
> I'LL DECIDE WHAT COUNTS.

> *(A* **COLLEGE STUDENT** *with a clipboard emerges from the* **CROWD**.*)*

COLLEGE STUDENT. Excuse me, have you got a minute for *Greenpeace*?

ZACK. *(Without breaking stride.)* Not right now. Taxi!

COLLEGE STUDENT. *(Approaching someone else.)* Excuse me, have you got a minute for *Greenpeace*?

> *(The* **CROWD** *sweeps* **ZACK** *and the* **COLLEGE STUDENT** *off, revealing a...)*

Newspaper Kiosk, Upper West Side

> (**HELEN**, *a slightly vacant-looking senior citizen, sits in a wheelchair while* **HYACINTH**, *her Jamaican attendant, reads lottery numbers written in the margins of* The Daily News *to the kiosk* **TICKET SELLER**.)

HYACINTH. Sixteen, thirty-eight, forty-eight, box six, box fifteen twice –

HELEN. Hyacinth –

HYACINTH. Not right now, sweetheart –

> (*She continues rattling off numbers as lights come up on the suggestion of an elevator. A* **CROWD OF NEW YORKERS** *hustles across the stage again. Several wear lab coats or hospital scrubs. They enter the elevator, which is in...*)

A Corridor At Roosevelt Hospital

> *(The elevator "dings" and the doors begin to slide closed as* **NEIL** *– mid-twenties, wearing hospital scrubs – rushes on, followed by* **CINDY***, also mid-twenties, also wearing hospital scrubs.* **CINDY** *is Chinese-American.)*

NEIL. Hold it, please! Hold the elevator!

> *(The elevator doors close.)*

Damnit!

> *(***NEIL*** *leans on the elevator button while* **CINDY** *studies the screen on her BlackBerry.)*

CINDY. O.K., I got the list –

NEIL. The what? Oh, "The List."

CINDY.
I'LL GET YOUR SUIT FROM THE CLEANERS.
YOU BUY A TIE FROM THE GAP.

NEIL.
AFTER I'M DONE AT THE DENTIST
WITH MY TEMPORARY CAP.

> *(Leaning on the button.)*

Where's the goddamn elevator?

CINDY.
YOU'LL TAKE THE CAR TO THE CARWASH.

NEIL.
YOU'RE GONNA BACK UP THE MAC.

CINDY.
AFTER I MAKE THE "CHAROSET" FOR THE SEDER –

> *(Her beeper beeps.)*

AND CALL YOUR MOTHER BACK.

She texted me in the middle of Mrs. Gilman's hip replacement to find out if my people eat matzoh.

NEIL. That's how she put it? "Your people?"

(*She shows him the message on her BlackBerry.*)

I'll call her. I'll tell her "your people" *invented* matzoh. Along with paper, printing, and gun powder, and – oh, yes – "The List."

CINDY. I thought we said we were gonna skip the Seder this year.

NEIL. Actually, I thought we said we were going to skip the August Moon Festival.

(**CINDY** *sighs; they retreat into their private thoughts.*)

CINDY.	NEIL
ANOTHER BRISKET STEWED IN KETCHUP.	WHEN DID IT ALL TURN WEIRD?
ANOTHER FLANKEN BOILED IN STOCK.	
	WHICH OF US DISAPPEARED?
ANOTHER GRANDPARENTAL INQUEST ON MY REPRODUCTIVE CLOCK.	
	LOST IN A
ANOTHER NIGHT OF ACID REFLUX.	LAUNDRY LIST –
ANOTHER WRINKLE IN MY BROW.	WE COEXIST SOMEHOW.

NEIL & CINDY.
WE COULD WORK OUT THE KINKS
IN THIS MARRIAGE IF TIME WOULD ALLOW –

(*"Ding!" as the elevator arrives and the elevator doors begin to slide open.*)

NEIL. *Finally*!

CINDY. We need some time for *us*, Neil.

NEIL. Absolutely –

   (As he guides her into the elevator.)

  JUST NOT RIGHT NOW...

   (Blackout, and lights up on the...)

Newspaper Kiosk

(...Where **HYACINTH** *continues to feed numbers to the* **TICKET SELLER**.*)*

HYACINTH. *(Giggling, now flirting with the* **TICKET SELLER**.*)* Fourteen, fifteen...

> *(***HYACINTH*** *inadvertently bumps* **HELEN***'s wheelchair. It begins to roll.)*

HELEN. Hyacinth!

HYACINTH. ...thirty-seven, box three ways twice –

HELEN. Hyacinth!

HYACINTH. In a minute, sweetheart –

HELEN. Hyacinth!

HYACINTH. *(Turns, sees* **HELEN** *rolling away.)* Oh, Lord, have mercy!

> *(***HYACINTH*** *rushes off after the wheelchair as a* **CROWD OF NEW YORKERS** *rushes on again. More hospital scrubs and lab coats. They bustle off, wiping the stage and revealing...)*
>
> *(***KEVIN***, early sixties and distinguished looking. He wears the buttoned-up uniform of a Park Avenue doorman. He is standing in a...)*

Hospital Emergency Room

> (*...Next to a very strung-out looking* **JUNKIE** *who is rocking back and forth and shaking.*)

KEVIN. You're shaking. You O.K.?

JUNKIE. My doctor thinks it's the caffeine. I think it's the heroin. What are you doing here?

KEVIN.
THURSDAY'S MY REGULAR TREATMENT.
HELL OF A YEAR THIS HAS BEEN.
EARLY THIS MORNING THE FEVER ROSE,
AND SO I THOUGHT,
"OH JEEZ, HERE GOES."
THERE WASN'T TIME TO CHANGE MY CLOTHES.
I HOPE THEY SQUEEZE ME IN.

> (*The* **JUNKIE** *doubles over, and starts rocking back and forth again. A* **NURSE** *approaches with a clipboard.*)

NURSE. Kevin O'Doherty?

KEVIN. That's me. But I think you ought to see this guy first.

NURSE. You're next.

KEVIN. I really think he needs to see somebody now.

> (*The* **NURSE** *shrugs and leads the* **JUNKIE** *off.* **KEVIN** *wipes his brow. Another* **CROWD OF NEW YORKERS** *rushes on, wiping the stage and revealing...*)

A Street Corner Someplace in Chelsea

(...Where **MAURICE** *[pronounced "Morris"] is waving for a taxi and talking on a cell phone.* **MAURICE** *is a high-end, socially connected interior decorator who looks like Andre Leon Talley and speaks with the lilting elegance of his Savannah roots. He is dressed impeccably – conservatively, but with a hint of flamboyance.)*

MAURICE. *(Into the phone.)*
YES, I REMEMBERED THE SWATCHES.
TOILE DE PROVENCE AND THEY'RE *FAB.*
SOON AS I GET OUT OF CHELSEA,
WE'LL HAVE BREAKFAST IF I EVER GET A CAB.

You know, in the old days they wouldn't pick me up cause I was black. Then they wouldn't pick me up cause I was gay. Now I think they won't pick me up because I voted for John McCain.

(Big booming laugh, then to himself.)

ANOTHER LITCHFIELD COUNTY POOL HOUSE.
ANOTHER INLAID PARQUET FLOOR.
ANOTHER ECO-FRIENDLY KITCHEN
FOR A SPREAD IN "ELLE DÉCOR."
ANOTHER DOGGIE BED IN MOHAIR
FOR AN EXTREMELY CHOOSEY CHOW...

Trust me, darling, when I'm finished with that pool house of yours it's going to look like the Petit Trianon, but with a plasma TV and a Jacuzzi.

(Another big laugh.)

On my way, darling!

(A kiss into the phone.)

MAURICE. *Mwa!*

    (He flips the phone shut.)

I WOULD SO LOVE TO GO
TO THE GEHRY MUSEUM IN BILBAO...
JUST NOT RIGHT NOW.

    (Steps into the street and waves.)

Taxi!

    (Lights up on...)

A Pedicab, Wheeling Through Traffic

(The **CABBIE** *is Pakistani, wearing a large set of headphones.* **ZACK** *sits in the back and is talking on the phone.)*

ZACK. No, I couldn't get a cab so I'm in one of those fucking bicycle things...Whose birthday?...Fine, get him one of those cards that says happy birthday from your uncle, stick a hundred bucks in it, and overnight it to him...No, no, tell him I'm going directly to the courthouse.

(To the **CABBIE.***)*

Federal Courthouse! Centre Street between Duane and Reade!

CABBIE. You want to go to *Duane-Reade*?

ZACK. Jesus –

(A horn and a clap of thunder. **ZACK** *jumps out of the pedicab into a rainstorm as another* **CROWD OF NEW YORKERS** *rushes on, all clutching umbrellas.)*

ZACK.	OTHERS.
RIGHT NOW,	AH
WITH WALL STREET IN	
DEMISE,	AH
THE THOUGHT OF SETTLING	
DOWN	AH
IS NOT THE WAY TO	
RISE.	AH

(Another burst of thunder and rain. **ZACK** *steps under an umbrella being held by a woman standing next to him.)*

ZACK.

> MY GOALS ARE AT HAND.
> MY MIND IS RESOLVED.
> IT'S SMARTER TO SURF THE WEB
> FOR A ONE-NIGHT STAND
> THAN TO GET "INVOLVED."

>> *(The* **CROWD** *breaks up. A* **SCRUFFY-LOOKING MAN** *holding a big plastic jug with a "UHO" sticker on it lurches after* **ZACK**.*)*

SCRUFFY-LOOKING MAN. Contribution for the Homeless? A penny? A dollar?

ZACK. Hey, hey –

> NOT RIGHT NOW.

>> *(***ZACK** *exits as lights come up on...)*

>> *(***ARLENE**, *a severe-looking radio talkshow host wearing a serious suit and carrying a serious-looking Ferragamo shoulder bag. She is at the front of the line at...)*

A Jamba Juice-Style Bar in Madison Square Park

> (...*Talking coldly into her cell phone and monitoring the preparation of her health drink, which is being methodically assembled by an affectless Hispanic woman wearing an incongruously cheery Madison Sq. Smoothie uniform and cap.*)

ARLENE. *(Into the phone.)* I understand it doesn't show up in your computer. If it did, I'd be in the limousine now, wouldn't I?

> *(Off the phone.)*

I asked for *extra* wheat germ –

> *(Back into the phone.)*

Hello? *Hello*?

> *(To the person on line behind her.)*

FIRST THEY FORGET YOUR APPOINTMENT.
THEN THEY MAROON YOU ON HOLD.
HAVING TO DEAL WITH THESE THIRD WORLD WORKERS
MAKES MY BLOOD RUN COLD.

> *(To the* **SMOOTHIE SALESWOMAN**.*)*

And no pitted fruits, I'm allergic –

> *(Back to the person on line behind her as the saleswoman deliberately tosses peach slices and the peach pit into the blender.)*

LOOK AT HER, SLOW AS MOLASSES,
PASSIVE AGGRESSIVE AND RUDE.
WHAT DOES SHE CARE IF MY INTERVIEW
WITH "CHRISTIAN YOUTH FOR ABSTINENCE" IS SCREWED?

> *(Back into the phone.)*

ARLENE.   I'm sorry?...I understand. Yes, of course. Fortunately, there *is* something more that *I* can do, which is to cancel my account and tell everybody why I'm doing it on my radio show this afternoon!

>   (*Snapping the phone closed.*)

Morons.

SMOOTHIE SALESWOMAN.   (*Handing her the drink.*) Have a nice day.

>   (**ARLENE** *shoots her a look and heads off, frowning at the headlines in her* New York Times.*)

ARLENE.

ANOTHER ANTI-FUR COAT PROTEST.

>   (*Looks up with smug satisfaction.*)

I THINK I'LL WEAR MY SILVER FOX.

>   (*Looks back at paper.*)

ANOTHER "SAVE-THE-PLANET" ACTOR
BACK IN CRYSTAL-METH DETOX.
OH, BUT IT'S GOOD TO BE THE SHOCK-JOCK
WHO ALL THE LEFTIES LOVE TO HATE.
LET 'EM ALL POP A STITCH
WHEN THIS RADIO BITCH SETS 'EM STRAIGHT!

>   (*A self-satisfied chortle.*)

HA!

>   (*She takes a big aggressive slurp of her drink as another* **CROWD OF NEW YORKERS** *trundles on, wiping the stage and revealing...*)

A Bank of Turnstiles in a Subway Station

(An attractive **YOUNG WOMAN** *enters carrying a couple of shopping bags from Whole Foods.)*

*(***ZACK*** *races on, heading for the turnstiles, and crashes into her. One of the bags breaks and clementines roll everywhere.)*

ZACK. Oh, shit –

(He starts to bend down to pick them up when we hear the sound of an arriving train. **ZACK** *looks at his watch, looks at the clementines, takes out a ten-dollar bill.)*

Ten bucks enough?

YOUNG WOMAN. What would be enough is if you helped me pick them up.

ZACK. Fine. Here's twenty.

(He throws her a twenty-dollar bill and dashes off through another set of turnstiles.)

YOUNG WOMAN. Asshole.

(The **YOUNG WOMAN** *collects her clementines and exits.* **ZACK** *finds himself on an empty subway platform, waiting for the train.)*

ZACK.
IT'S JUST ANOTHER NEW YORK MONDAY.
ALREADY HALF AN HOUR BEHIND.
WHATEVER LINE THIS IS,
I'M GETTIN' ON THE FIRST TRAIN THAT I FIND.
YOU WANNA MAKE IT UP THE LADDER,
YOU MAKE A SINGLEMINDED VOW.

ZACK.

> YOU'RE A RAT IN THE RACE,
> YOU'RE A PAWN IN THE GAME HERE.
> KEEP UP THE PACE,
> IT'S THE REASON YOU CAME HERE.
> CHASING THE BUCK
> OR THE YEN OR THE EURO,
> SOMEDAY I KNOW
> I'LL BE HAPPY AS HELL, SOMEHOW...
> JUST NOT –

OTHERS.

> NOT QUITE –

ZACK & OTHERS.

> NOT QUITE RIGHT NOW!

Entering the Subway Car

[INSTRUMENTAL "SUBWAY CAR"]

(Squeals, beeps, and bells, as the subway car arrives and the doors slide open. Arrayed around the inside of the car are **MIGUEL, GINA, NEIL, CINDY, MAURICE, KEVIN, ARLENE,** *and* **HELEN** – *in her wheelchair, but without* **HYACINTH***. The wheelchair is hooked into a special spot where the seating flips up to accommodate it.)*

*(***CINDY** *is doing hospital paperwork.* **NEIL** *has fallen asleep on her shoulder.* **MIGUEL** *is playing a video game on his cell phone. His messenger bag is on the floor beside him.* **KEVIN** *is reading* The Daily News. **GINA***, iPod earphones plugged in her ears, is flipping through a copy of* Vogue. **ARLENE** *is reading the* Times. **MAURICE** *is simply staring.)*

(More beeps and bells as the doors start to slide closed. At the last possible moment, **ZACK** *dashes on and thrusts his briefcase through the closing doors.)*

ZACK. Come on, come on, come on...

(Finally the doors spring open and **ZACK** *tumbles into the car. No one pays any attention. Then the doors slide closed and the train begins to move.)*

*(***ZACK** *hangs on to a pole, too wired to sit. A beat, then the train lurches, the outer shell of the car is pulled off, exposing the interior of the car – which stops.)*

ZACK. CINDY. KEVIN. MIGUEL. MAURICE. GINA. ARLENE.
Shit... Great... Jesus... *Whoa*... Lord...   Hey! Of
                                                       course...

*(Lights dim on the interior of the car, come up
down-stage on a Subway Trainman, in his
early forties, apparently tucked into his...)*

Compartment at the Front of the Train

(His name is **STANLEY***. He picks up a PA microphone.)*

STANLEY. Ladies and Gentlemen, this is your Trainman speaking...

[MUSIC NO. 3 - "BLIPS"]

(His speech degenerates into unintelligible gibberish.)

...and we expect to have you on your way shortly.

*(***NEIL***, who has been asleep on* **CINDY***'s shoulder, wakes up.)*

NEIL. What happened?

CINDY. I don't know. We stopped.

NEIL. Where are we?

CINDY. I think the last station was Eighty-first Street.

MIGUEL. Yo, this is the Two, baby. The Two doesn't stop at Eighty-first Street.

NEIL. This is the *Two?*

(He looks perplexed, as **STANLEY** *removes his work gloves.)*

STANLEY.
HERE WE GO AGAIN.
TRAPPED WITH THE DEMENTOS
ON THE SUBWAY RIDE FROM HELL.

ZACK. *(To himself.)* I don't have time for this...

STANLEY.
> FEET BEGIN TO TWITCH.
> SYMPHONIES OF BITCHING
> HAVE BEGUN TO RISE AND SWELL.

ZACK. *(Looking at his watch.)* I definitely do not have time for this.

STANLEY.
> COUGHS AND SIGHS AND GRUMBLES.
> SOCIAL ORDER CRUMBLES
> AS THE CAPTIVE PISS AND MOAN.

NEIL. I'm going to miss the dentist –

> *(**ZACK** drums his fingers on his briefcase;
> **GINA** hums to her iPod; **NEIL** tries to text
> message on his PDA.)*

STANLEY.
> THE ATTACHE-CASE-DRUMMER.
> THE EARPLUG-IPOD-HUMMER,
> TEXTING ON A QUAD-BAND PHONE.

KEVIN. T-Mobile?

> *(**NEIL** nods.)*

My condolences.

STANLEY.
> SOMEONE DUE IN COURT
> GROUSES SELF-IMPORTANTLY
> HIS ASS IS ON THE LINE.

ZACK. *(Checking his watch again.)* I have to deliver this summation.

STANLEY.
> TYPIC'LY BY NOW,
> SOMEONE'S COUNTING VOWELS
> IN THE ACNE DOCTOR'S SIGN.

CINDY. Sixteen...seventeen...eighteen...

STANLEY.
> DON'T THE DOTS CONNECT?
> HAVE THEY NO PERSPECTIVE
> HOW MINUTELY SMALL THEY ARE?
> THE TRAIN OF LIFE MOVES ON.
> WHAT ARE WE WHEN IT'S GONE?
> BLIPS ... ON THE COSMIC RADAR.

HELEN. Hyacinth...?

STANLEY.
> MERE BLIPS OF STRAY ELECTRONS
> ACROSS A VAST GALACTIC SCREEN.
> BIG DEAL, I MADE YOU MISS YOUR DENTIST.
> ANOTHER BLOW TO ORAL HYGIENE.
> LOST SHIPS WITHOUT SAFE HARBOR
> UPON AN INTERSTELLAR SEA.
> WHO CARES, YOU'RE LATE FOR YOUR APPOINTMENT.
> WE'RE FLIES IN TIME'S PRIMORDIAL OINTMENT.

> *(Increasingly irksome buzzes and beeps are emitted by the video game* **MIGUEL** *is playing on his cell phone.)*

> NEXT YOU MAY DEPEND
> SOMEONE PLAYS NINTENDO
> JUST TO HELP MAKE MATTERS WORSE.

MIGUEL. Level three! Aw-right!

STANLEY.
> SOMEONE TAKES HER CUE,
> DIGGING FOR WELLBUTRIN
> IN THE BLACK HOLE OF HER PURSE.

ARLENE. It's gotta be in here...

> *(***HELEN*** *looks around, confused and lost.)*

STANLEY.
> HERE WE HAVE THE GRANNY
> SEARCHING FOR HER NANNY.
> HARD TO FIND A GOOD R.N.

HELEN. Hyacinth...?

> (**NEIL***'s breathing becomes labored.*)

STANLEY.
> THE HYPER-VENTILATOR.
> THE TRAIN RE-DECORATOR,
> CHANGING THE DÉCOR AGAIN.

MAURICE. This train is in desperate need of window treatments.

STANLEY.
> DRIPPING WITH DISDAIN,
> SOMEONE STARTS COMPLAINING
> THAT THE TRANSIT UNION STINKS.

ARLENE. Worse than the Air Traffic Controllers.

STANLEY.
> HERE'S A HELPFUL HINT:
> I'M NOT FRIGGIN' INT'RESTED
> WHAT EV'RY AIRHEAD THINKS.

GINA. This *never* happens on the Paris Metro.

STANLEY.
> WHO SAID LIFE WAS FAIR?
> HOW DOES YOURS COMPARE
> TO SOME GAZILLION-YEAR-OLD STAR?
> WHAT *ARE* WE IN THE END?
> EPHEMERAL, MY FRIEND.
> BLIP...

NEIL. Damn!

STANLEY.
> BLIP...

ZACK. Shit!

STANLEY.
  BLIP...

HELEN. Hyacinth...?

ALL. She isn't here!

STANLEY.
  BLIPS...ON THE COSMIC RADAR.

       (**STANLEY** *exits.*)

ZACK. *(Knocking on the door to the Trainman's compartment at the front of the car.)* Hey. Hey –!

KEVIN. I don't think there's anybody in there –

ZACK. *(Sharply.)* I gotta be in court in forty minutes, O.K.?

NEIL. This cap –

       (**NEIL** *puts* **CINDY**'s *finger in his mouth.*)

  Feel how loose that is? It could fall off. I could *swallow* it. I cannot miss this appointment.

MIGUEL. You know, with all due respect, you uptight white boys gotta learn to chill out.

NEIL. Some of us uptight white boys have responsibilities, you know? Things we actually have to do.

MIGUEL. Hey, I'm just saying, getting all Hebrew and agitated isn't gonna make the train move –

NEIL. "Hebrew and agitated?" What's that supposed to mean?

CINDY. Please.

NEIL. O.K., O.K., but you're the one who makes the lists, all right? And we're due back in the E.R. in twelve hours.

MIGUEL. So you'll be back in thirteen hours. There's worse things in life than being late for work.

MAURICE. Like in your case, I suspect, being *on time* for work.

ARLENE. Ha!

>　(**MIGUEL** *clutches his chest like he's been shot in the heart, then grins.* **GINA** *stares at* **MAURICE**.)

GINA. Excuse me, but I know that voice. Aren't you Maurice Hathaway?

MAURICE. Darling, I am.

GINA. I thought so! What are you doing on the *subway*?

MAURICE. Same thing you are, darling. Sitting here and trying not to scream.

GINA. Isn't it *awful*? I don't know why anybody travels this way! You know, I absolutely love your work –

>　(*Indicating her open copy of* Vogue.)

This house you just did for Annette de la Renta – it's fantastic.

MAURICE. Do me a favor, darling. Call *Mr.* de la Renta. Tell *him* that.

GINA. *(Laughs.)* You know I'm probably wrong, I had had three or four Bellinis, but I think we met at Fashion Week last year in Milan.

MAURICE. I wasn't there last year, darling.

GINA. Then I guess I'd had four or *five* Bellini's.

>　(**MAURICE** *chuckles.* **MIGUEL** *snatches the magazine from* **GINA** *and hoists it in triumph.*)

MIGUEL. Hey, check it out, my man's in the magazine for real! "Internationally acclaimed designer Maurice –

(He pronounces it "Moe-reece.")

– Hathaway!"

MAURICE. It's pronounced Morris.

MIGUEL. Come on, I got a cousin named Maurice.

MAURICE. Morris.

MIGUEL. S'pose I just call you "Mo," O.K.?

HELEN. *(Eyeing Kevin's doorman outfit.)* A man in uniform. Good for you.

CINDY. You think the old woman is O.K.?

ARLENE. She's fine. She's lucky. She doesn't know where the hell she is.

   *(To **MAURICE**.)*

You know, if and when the unionized sub-literates who operate this transit system finally get this train moving, I'd like to have you on my show.

MIGUEL. You got a show? She's got a show?

GINA. I thought so! "Talking Straighter with Arlene Slater," right?

MIGUEL. Come on. This chick is Arlene Slater?! Man, this is like the celebrity express!

NEIL. She's a pig –

CINDY. *Neil* –

NEIL. Excuse me, but you're a pig.

ARLENE. *(To **NEIL**.)* Thank you for sharing.

MIGUEL. Oooh...

ARLENE. *(Back to **MAURICE**.)* Anyway, I saw your name in an article in *Commentary* about prominent gay men who oppose same sex marriage. I would love to have you come on the program and talk about your reasons.

MAURICE. My reasons, darling? Well, I can tell you this: they've got everything to do with the fact that two people do not need a bogus piece of paper to validate their relationship and nothing to do with the fag-bashing crap I hear coming out of that poisonous radio program of yours.

ARLENE. I wish I could understand your point of view. I just can't get my head that far up my ass.

ZACK. *(Peering through a window.)* The hell with this, I can't see anything! Who tried the other end? Did *anybody* try the other end?

> *(He strides to the other end of the car and tries to pull the door open. It doesn't move. He tries harder.)*

KEVIN. The next car's not going to move any sooner than this one.

ZACK. A physics lesson. Thanks.

KEVIN. I only meant –

ZACK. I know what you meant.

KEVIN. Hey. Bad joke, O.K.? Everyone's a little tense. I know I am –

> *(Extending his hand.)*

By the way, my name is Kevin –

> *(A sudden buzz, the lights flicker and snap off.)*

> *(Blackout. Through the darkness, reactions from everybody, ranging from anxiety to anger. Then another buzz as emergency lights come back on, but dimly.)*

> *(**STANLEY** is now standing in the car, holding his clipboard and a crowbar. Everyone jumps.)*

STANLEY. Sorry. I scared you.

ZACK. Jesus. Where the hell did you come from?

NEIL. What's going on?

GINA. *(Overlapping.)* What happened?

STANLEY. Power's gone. All we've got left are these emergency lights.

ARLENE. Christ –

NEIL. Well, how soon are we going to move?

MIGUEL. And don't tell me: "The train is being held by the dispatcher, we'll be –"

STANLEY. *(Cutting him off.)* I can't reach the dispatcher. The radio went out with the power.

CINDY. You mean we're cut off?

STANLEY. That's the way it looks.

ARLENE. I don't believe this –

ZACK. I've gotta be in court in half an hour –!

NEIL. *(Simultaneously.)* I got a temporary cap! I'm due at the dentist –!

ARLENE. *(Simultaneously.)* I've got a breakfast meeting at the Café des Artistes –!

STANLEY. *(Cutting through.)* I understand, what can I say? But you know, you should count your blessings. I've had cars stop on me with forty people in 'em and no air conditioning. There's only eight of you.

HELEN. Nine.

STANLEY. What?

CINDY. She's right. There's nine of us.

STANLEY. *(Frowning, looking around, then at his clipboard.)* Nine...Anyway, for the moment, all we can do is sit tight.

MAURICE. These are New Yorkers, darling. They are not accustomed to "sitting tight."

NEIL. *(Quietly.)* What if something happened?

ZACK. You mean like what if the train we're on broke down?

NEIL. No, I mean something else.

ARLENE. I know what he means. He means like 9/11.

GINA. *(Anxiously.)* 9/11?

NEIL. Right. And we're trapped down here and no one knows we're here and there's nobody to come and get us.

KEVIN. Anything like that, I'm sure we would have heard, right?

STANLEY. Maybe. Not necessarily.

CINDY. Not necessarily?

STANLEY. Well, the deepest tunnels in the system go down almost fifty feet –

ZACK. So you're saying what? A bomb could go off and we wouldn't hear?

STANLEY. Well, I've never actually been down here when a bomb went off –

ARLENE. This is ridiculous –

> *(She stands abruptly, yanks her phone out of her bag and tries to get a signal.* **MIGUEL** *does the same.)*

MIGUEL. You got any bars? How many bars you got?

ARLENE. Shut up.

> *(***ARLENE*** *shoves the phone back in her bag as* **NEIL** *starts to breath heavily again.)*

CINDY. Are you O.K.?

NEIL. You're always asking me that. *Yes*, I'm O.K. I'm fine –

ZACK. *(To the* **STANLEY**.*)* So just to sum up. You get a salary, benefits, a pension, and in an emergency you haven't got the slightest idea what to do, is that right?

STANLEY. I'm open to suggestions.

ZACK. Great –

> (**ZACK** *strides to the sliding doors, bangs on the glass.*)

Hey! *Hey*!

KEVIN. I can't see anything. The lights must still be out –

ZACK. *(To* **STANLEY**.*)* Open them.

STANLEY. I can't. Not between stations.

NEIL. *(Breathing heavily.)* We gotta get outta here –

CINDY. You heard him, honey, we have to sit –

NEIL. We gotta get outta here!

GINA. Is he all right?

CINDY. *(Urgently patting the pockets in* **NEIL**'s *backpack.)* Yeah, he's great. Where is it, Neil? Where's the inhaler?!

> (*She finds it, guides it to* **NEIL**'s *mouth; he pumps, inhales, then lets out a long, slow breath...*)

NEIL. *(To* **CINDY**, *without meeting her eye.)* Thank you...

GINA. I was only going to ask if I could help.

CINDY. How? By buying him a Bellini during Fashion Week?

KEVIN. Look, I know it's a cliché, but the best thing we can do is stay –

ZACK. The hell with this. How far to the next station?

STANLEY. Hard to say. If I knew exactly –

ZACK. *How far?*

STANLEY. Five, maybe six blocks.

ZACK. Right. So here's the plan. We get these doors to open and we head down the tunnel until we get to the next station. If there's no one in the station, we go up top and find out what's going on.

STANLEY. You know, the third rail –

ZACK. *(Sharply.)* I know all about the third rail –

> *(Leaning in and looking at* **STANLEY***'s badge.)*

– "Stanley." Thanks for your help. O.K., who's coming?

MIGUEL. The man's advice was to sit tight.

CINDY. *(Indicating* **HELEN***.)* Someone's gotta stay with her.

HELEN. You know those sticks you use? For picking up the egg rolls? I could never get the hang of those things.

ARLENE. All right. O.K.

NEIL. *(To* **CINDY***.)* I think I should probably go –

CINDY. I think you should stay with me.

GINA. I don't think anyone should go. I think we should stay here and wait for help.

ARLENE. Help from *who*? We need to help ourselves!

KEVIN. I'll go.

ARLENE. So will I.

ZACK. O.K., then –

> *(To* **STANLEY***.)*

These doors – there must be a release. Some kind of button, or a switch –

(He looks around for it, points to the crowbar
STANLEY *is holding.)*

Give me that.

STANLEY. That's official MTA equipment –

ZACK. *(Snatching it.)* Asshole...

*(***ZACK** *shoves the crowbar between the doors*
and leans on it. **KEVIN** *helps him.)*

STANLEY. *(To himself.)* Waste of time.

HELEN. Why are they doing that?

CINDY. They're trying to get out.

HELEN. *(To* **CINDY.***)* Sometimes, like with a dumpling, I'd
try to use one as a spear.

(The doors don't move.)

ZACK. *Shit*! Shit! Shit! Shit!

MAURICE. I have to tell you, I did not expect to pass
my last moment on earth in a space as indifferently
decorated as a New York City subway car.

ZACK. This is not going to be anybody's last moment
on earth!

STANLEY. He's right, actually, it's not.

NEIL. It's not?! How the hell do you know?!

KEVIN. Listen, I think we should all –

ARLENE. How about *worst* moment on earth, could we
agree on that?

STANLEY. *(Chuckling.)* Well, I don't guess this would be
anybody's idea of a *perfect* moment.

ZACK. Listen to him, he's amused. Trapped in a subway
car? No, I don't guess it would.

STANLEY. But what about that? What *would* be your idea of a perfect moment? I mean, we're going to be here for a while. If you had to look back at your life, consider all the –

MIGUEL. What are you? The Dali fuckin' Lama? "Look back at your life. Find a perfect moment."

STANLEY. Hey, listen, I'm just saying –

NEIL. *(Starting to lose it.)* We all heard what you're just saying. Now we want you to shut up and get us the hell out of here.

CINDY. Neil –

ARLENE. No, he's right. You want a perfect moment? This would be a perfect moment for you to do your goddamn job.

> *(**NEIL** grabs the crowbar, starts to beat it against the door.)*

KEVIN. Hey, easy –

CINDY. Neil, stop it!

ARLENE. Don't stop him, help him!

NEIL. Come on! Come on! *Come on* –!

HELEN. *(Anxiously.)* Hyacinth!

STANLEY. *(Overlapping.)* You know that glass is –

NEIL. Shut up!

STANLEY. Fine. But you're only –

> *(**NEIL** wheels around, aims a blow at **STANLEY**.)*

ZACK.	CINDY.	GINA.	ARLENE.	HELEN.
Jesus!	*Neil*!	Hey, stop him!	Grab it!	*Hyacinth*!

MIGUEL. Wait, wait, wait! *I got it!*

> *(Everything stops. **KEVIN** grabs the crowbar away from **NEIL**.)*

MAURICE. Excuse me, you've got what?

MIGUEL. That thing he said. My perfect moment!

> *(Ad-lib reactions: "For Christ's sakes." "Oh, Jesus" "Oh, come on...")*

No, no. For real. Listen to this...Montefiore Hospital, the Bronx. I'm finishing a run – dropping off some X-rays or something – and I'm about to hop back on my bike when suddenly, she appears. Nurse Angelique Rodriguez. A vision, like an angel descended from the ceiling of the Sistine Chapel. It was beautiful. I throw her a little smile...and next thing I know we're in the janitor's closet, knockin' over mops and brooms, yo, and this chick is giving me a "happy ending!"

ARLENE. What's a "happy ending?"

MIGUEL. In the Bronx, baby, it's what we call a blow job.

ARLENE. Give me the crowbar –

> *(She reaches for it. A scuffle. **MIGUEL** jumps up on the seat at the far end of the car. Chaos. Suddenly, **HELEN** cuts through the hub-bub.)*

HELEN. September fourteenth, nineteen forty-four –

> *(Everybody turns and stares.)*

CINDY. What was that?

GINA. What did she say?

STANLEY. Helen...?

[MUSIC NO. 3A BEFORE "FLIBBERTY"]

HELEN. *(To* **STANLEY.**) I had a moment, too. The kind that you talked about – a perfect moment.

STANLEY. You had a moment on September fourteenth, nineteen forty-four?

CINDY. How did he know her name was Helen?

ARLENE. How did *she* know her name was Helen?

HELEN. They had just opened up a new USO, right next to the library. You know the big one downtown?

STANLEY. Downtown in...?

HELEN. Buffalo, where I grew up.

ARLENE. You know, I think I can get a radio program out of this. "The Greatest Generation Remembers!" But not much.

> *(Ad-libs: Hey, give her a break... She's an old lady... Don't be so nasty...)*

KEVIN. Listen, any minute now somebody's going to figure out we're missing. I think we should all just settle down.

ZACK. *(Looking at his watch.)* I am totally screwed.

HELEN. *(Continuing, to* **STANLEY.**) The War was on, and I was training to be a nurse. It was a scary job, and every now and then I just had to cut loose or I'd bust, you know? Anyway, I had a girlfriend, and the two of us, we loved to dance. So first chance we got, off we went to that new USO –

[MUSIC NO. 4 "FLIBBERTY JIBBERS AND THE WOBBLY KNEES"]

(Swing-time music erupts as lights bump up on...)

A U.S.O. Dance Hall, 1944

(A dance-band, pretty lights, and Dancing Couples – **SOLDIERS** *and their* **GIRLS**. *Fronting the band are* **TWO VOCALISTS**, *a* **MAN** *and a* **WOMAN**.)*

*(***YOUNG HELEN*** hurries on, done up in a wartime frock and hair-do. She is fiddling with the buttons on her blouse. Her* **GIRLFRIEND** *spots her, breaks away from her partner.)*

GIRLFRIEND. Helen, honey, where you been?!

YOUNG HELEN. I'm here, aren't I?!

(Struggling with the buttons.)

Tch. Me and my fidgety fingers!

GIRLFRIEND. Aw, you just got the flibberty-jibbers. Now quit fussin', you look delish –

(A handsome **YOUNG SOLDIER** *enters.)*

Ten-hut!

HELEN. And that's when I saw him, and he saw me.

(The **SOLDIER** *stops and stares at* **YOUNG HELEN**. *She stares back. It's love at first sight.)*

SOLDIER. Excuse me, Miss? Do you suppose I could have this dance?

*(***YOUNG HELEN*** nods. They begin to dance.)*

(N.B. During the following, the interior of the subway car should all but disappear. All we need to know at the moment is that we are inside a remembered moment, inside **HELEN**'s *head.)*

MALE VOCALIST.
FLIBBERTY JIBBERS

FEMALE VOCALIST.
AND WOBBLY KNEES.

BOTH VOCALISTS.
EVEN THE BIRDS AND BEES
HAVE HEEBIE-JEEBIES.
SUGAR, YOU TURN ME TO COTTAGE CHEESE –

MALE VOCALIST.
WITH FLIBBERTY-JIBBERTY-JIBBERS...

FEMALE VOCALIST.
AND WOBBLY KNEES.

GIRLFRIEND. *(Over her shoulder, as she dances past*
YOUNG HELEN.*)* War may be hell, Sister, but heaven is
a man in uniform!

FEMALE VOCALIST.
FIDGETY FINGERS

MALE VOCALIST.
AND TWO LEFT FEET.

BOTH VOCALISTS.
HOW CAN I SWING THE BEAT
OF BOOGIE-WOOGIE
KNOWIN' YOU'RE GOIN' TO JOIN THE FLEET

MALE VOCALIST.
WITH FIDGETY-FIDGETY FINGERS...

FEMALE VOCALIST.
AND TWO LEFT FEET.

YOUNG HELEN. You dance very nicely.

SOLDIER. My sister taught me. She said we had to beat the
Nazis everywhere, including on the dance floor.

VOCALISTS.

> I SAW YOU AND *ZING*.
> YOU TUCKED ME UNDER YOUR WING.
> IN YOUR ARMS
> SO STRONG AND CAPABLE,
> CUPID'S CHARMS
> ARE INESCAPBLE.

SOLDIER. By the way, my name is –

YOUNG HELEN. Tommy. Tommy Mathis.

> *(He looks perplexed; she points at his name tag.)*

It's on your chest.

TOMMY. *(Grinning, embarrassed.)* Sure it is.

YOUNG HELEN & HELEN. *(As* **HELEN** *stands.)* And mine's Helen.

VOCALISTS.

> TICKETY-TOCK LIKE A METRONOME,
> KEEPIN' MY HEART AT HOME
> TO PASS THE MOMENTS
> KNITTIN' A SWEATER WITH AUNT LOUISE,
> DREAMIN' OF YOU OVERSEAS

MALE VOCALIST.

> WITH TICKETY-TOCKETY

FEMALE VOCALIST.

> FLUTTERY-FLITTERY

MALE VOCALIST.

> BIPPITY-BOPPITY

FEMALE VOCALIST.

> JIMINY-JITTERY

BOTH.

> FLIBBERTY-JIBBERTY-JIBBERS
> AND WOBBLY KNEES.

(Dance break. The subway doors open and **HELEN** *leaves the car and appears in the USO. She watches* **TOMMY** *and her younger self.)*

HELEN. My God, would you look at me? I really *did* look delish!

*(***YOUNG HELEN*** *and* **TOMMY** *continue to dance.)*

TOMMY. I'd like to ask you something...

(He hesitates; **YOUNG HELEN** *looks up at him.)*

I mean, I know we just met, and I'm shipping out first thing in the morning, so it really isn't fair, but...

(He pauses; she waits.)

HELEN. And then he just sort of stopped. I guess he got a little tongue-tied, so I gave him a little push.

YOUNG HELEN. I know they say loose lips sink ships, but you can trust me. Honest.

TOMMY. *(Smiles.)* O.K. then...would you be my girl?

HELEN. *(Stepping in to replace* **YOUNG HELEN**.*)* Yes, I will.

TOMMY. And will you wait for me?

HELEN. Yes, I'll wait for you.

(They dance...)

VOCALISTS.
DIZZY IN YOUR SWAY,
MY HEELS GO EV'RY WHICH WAY.

VOCALISTS.
WHEN YOUR EYES
LOOK DOWN AND DROWN IN ME,
BUTTERFLIES
GO UP AND DOWN IN ME.

*(***YOUNG HELEN*** joins* **TOMMY** *and* **HELEN**.
The three dance together for a moment, then
HELEN *breaks away.)*

HELEN. Two weeks later he was killed, on the beach at
Anzio. It took a long time, but I got over it. And I got
married and had a family and I had a good life. But
that one moment, when Tommy Mathis, Private First
Class, from Muncie, Indiana asked me to be his girl,
that was the most perfect moment of my life...

*(***YOUNG HELEN*** and* **TOMMY** *separate.*
TOMMY *smiles at* **HELEN** *and offers his open
arms, exactly as he did to* **YOUNG HELEN**.
HELEN *steps into them and they dance...)*

TICKETY-TOCK LIKE A METRONOME,
KEEPIN' MY HEART AT HOME
TO PASS THE MOMENTS
KNITTIN' A SWEATER WITH AUNT LOUISE,
DREAMIN' OF YOU OVERSEAS –
WITH...

WOMEN & HELEN.
TICKETY-TOCKETY

MEN.
FLUTTERY-FLITTERY

WOMEN & HELEN.
BIPPITY-BOPPITY

MEN.
JIMINY-JITTERY

WOMEN & HELEN.
FIDGETY FINGERS

ALL.
AND FEVERISH FLUSHES
AND FLIBBERTY JIBBERS
AND WOBBLY KNEES!

(The USO and everybody in it vanishes, as **TOMMY**, **HELEN** *and* **YOUNG HELEN** *dance off together – and disappear...)*

(Lights back up on the subway car. **HELEN**'s *wheelchair is empty.)*

KEVIN. Where is she?

GINA. Where'd she go?

STANLEY. Well, I'm guessing, but I'll bet she's dancing at the USO in Buffalo in the Fall of 1944.

MIGUEL. *(A sudden grin.)* And I'm guessing that someplace around here there's a hidden camera.

STANLEY. A hidden camera?

MIGUEL. Come on. This is one of those shows, right?

ZACK. *(Ignoring him.)* She must have gone into another car.

NEIL. She was in a wheelchair. How could she go into another car?

MIGUEL. *(To* **STANLEY**.*)* Where's the camera? Up here? No?

(Pointing to another part of the subway car.)

Behind the *Dr. Z* ad?

*(***STANLEY** *ignores him.)*

That's it. I got it, right?

(He grins, suddenly erupts with ham-actor histrionics.)

MIGUEL. Oh, my God! The Old Lady! She disappeared! What the fuck happened to the Old Lady?!

ZACK. *(Staring through the window at the end of the car.)* There is no other car. No car and no tracks. It's like we're nowhere.

NEIL. *(To* **STANLEY.***)* What's happening to us?

PASSENGERS. *(Variously, simultaneously.)* What's going on?! What is this?!... Where the hell are we?!... What happened to the train?!

STANLEY. Let me ask *you* a question. Anyone of you –

(*To* **ARLENE.***)*

What train are you on?

ARLENE. What *train?*

PASSENGERS. What *train?!*... Who cares what train?!... What difference does *that* make?!

STANLEY. *(To* **ARLENE.***)* What train?

ARLENE. I'm on the N, going uptown.

MIGUEL. You're going uptown, baby, but you're not on the N. You're on the Two.

KEVIN. I'm on the One, the Broadway Local, coming home from – except, no, I stopped at the E.R.

CINDY. We're on the C.

MAURICE. Frankly, darling, I don't know what train I'm on. The last thing I remember before I found myself sitting here was trying to hail a taxi.

STANLEY. So you don't remember waiting on the platform, or getting on the train?

(**MAURICE** *shakes his head.*)

Does anybody?

ZACK. Yeah. I knocked somebody down –

STANLEY. *(Ignoring him, to* **GINA.***)* What's the last thing you remember before you found yourself sitting here?

GINA. I was standing on the corner in front of this construction site. I was waiting for the light to change...

STANLEY. And then?

GINA. And then someone started shouting and I heard a roaring noise...

STANLEY. Which would have been the crane supports collapsing.

> *(To* **NEIL** *and* **CINDY.***)*

And you two, you were waiting for an elevator –

CINDY. We were arguing a little bit. The doors opened, we went in...

NEIL. But I don't remember coming out.

STANLEY. *(Lifting the messenger bag off the floor.)* You, Miguel. What's in the bag?

MIGUEL. Trust me, you don't want to mess around with what's in the bag –

> *(He grabs it. The bag is empty.)*

Oh, Jesus. Uncle Manny is gonna kill me.

STANLEY. Unless maybe the M4 bus on Fort Washington Avenue beat him to it...Arlene? "No pitted fruit...?"

ARLENE. I'm allergic.

GINA. I don't get this. What's he saying? I was in an accident?

MAURICE. What he's saying, darling, is that all of us are dead.

GINA. Dead? I'm *dead*?

MIGUEL. Yeah, you know? Like in *The Twilight Zone.* "Beep, boop, beep, beep. Beep, boop, beep, beep."

> *(Ad-libs: Dismissive disbelief.)*

CINDY. Neil – try the stethoscope.

STANLEY. Good idea. Give it a try.

*(**NEIL** pulls the stethoscope from around his neck and listens to his chest. He moves it around with increasing urgency. **CINDY** takes the ear pieces out of his ears, puts them in hers and listens...)*

MAURICE. So then this would be what? Purgatory? Hell? Not even Duke Ellington thought the A Train went to Heaven.

STANLEY. This would be what comes next.

*(Ad-lib protestations from the **PASSENGERS**.)*

Look, I know this is a lot to take in. Fifteen minutes ago you were sitting in a stalled subway car and your biggest problem was whether or not you were going to miss your dentist's appointment. But this, this journey – this is what comes next.

(More vocal protestations.)

Not always on a subway train. Different people make the trip in different ways. But everybody makes it – and everybody gets a chance, one chance, to pick a perfect moment from their lives and to live in that moment for eternity.

KEVIN. So you're saying the old lady –

STANLEY. Helen.

KEVIN. She really is dancing at a USO in Buffalo?

CINDY. I don't buy any of it –

ARLENE. Neither do I.

NEIL. If we fell down an elevator shaft, where's all the blood?

GINA. And broken bones?

MIGUEL. I got killed chasing a *chicken*? Fuck that!

NEIL. Look at us! We're fine!

ZACK. I know *I* am.

KEVIN. I'm not –

> *(The hub-bub stops.)*

I have cancer. I've had chemo and radiation. Nothing's worked. I spiked a fever, that's what I was doing at the E.R. –

STANLEY. Where you had a seizure, by the way.

> **(KEVIN** *looks at him.)*

KEVIN.   Anyway, I've thought about this stuff. Looked back at my life. The good moments and the bad ones. At what mattered and what didn't…My father was a doorman, too – at one of those big buildings on Fifth Avenue. He was a Giants fan, so naturally, so was I. So it's 1954, I'm nine years old, and the Giants are getting ready to play the Cleveland Indians in the World Series –

Young Kevin's Apartment, The Bronx, 1954

[MUSIC NO. 5 "THE BEST SEATS IN THE BALLPARK"]

*(***YOUNG KEVIN***, age nine, enters. So does his* **DAD***, wearing a doorman's uniform and carrying a lunchbox.)*

YOUNG KEVIN. Hey, Dad, how was work?

KEVIN'S DAD. *(Offhand.)* Good, good. Say, Kevin, I thought I might ask for Tuesday off so we could listen to the ballgame together, what d'you say?

YOUNG KEVIN. Jeez, Dad, that'd be great.

KEVIN'S DAD. Yeah. And I have a special place where I thought we might listen to it. Because Mr. Winston, who lives in the penthouse at ten thirty-five, he's got a pair of tickets right behind the Giants dugout and it turns out he can't use 'em –

YOUNG KEVIN. Wait. Are you saying –?

KEVIN'S DAD. *(Beaming.)* Laddie, you and me are going to the opening game of the 1954 World Series!

*(***YOUNG KEVIN*** *shrieks with joy.)*

WE'LL GET THERE REALLY EARLY.
ELEVEN AT THE LATEST.

YOUNG KEVIN.
IN TIME FOR BATTIN' PRACTICE.

KEVIN'S DAD.
WE'LL LEAVE AT HALF-PAST TEN.

YOUNG KEVIN.
WE GOTTA BUY A PROGRAM.
GET WILLIE MAYS TO SIGN IT –
'CUZ WILLIE, HE'S THE GREATEST.

GROWN KEVIN.
> THEN OR NOW.

KEVIN'S DAD.
> BRING YOUR PEN.

YOUNG KEVIN.
> WE'LL HAVE A COUPLE HOTDOGS –

KEVIN'S DAD.
> – THE FIRST PITCH OF THE INNING.

YOUNG KEVIN & HIS DAD.
> AND THEN JUST KEEP 'EM COMING
> IF THE GIANTS KEEP ON WINNING!

KEVIN'S DAD.
> A SIDE OF FRIES WITH KETCHUP
> WHILE THEY'RE CRISPY, FRESH AND HOT.

YOUNG KEVIN.
> NOT SOGGY LIKE THE BLEACHERS.

KEVIN'S DAD.
> KID, THE BLEACHERS THIS IS *NOT*.

GROWN KEVIN.
> WE GOT...THE BEST SEATS IN THE BALLPARK!
> SO CLOSE YOU ALMOST CAN FEEL IT.
> AND SEE IT. AND HEAR IT...

KEVIN'S DAD.
> THE WHOOSH OF A CURVE BALL.

YOUNG KEVIN.
> THE CRACK OF THE BAT.

BOTH.
> WE'VE NEVER BEEN CLOSER –

GROWN KEVIN.
> THE TWO OF US...

ALL THREE.

– THAN THAT.

AND WITH THE BEST FRICKIN' SEATS IN THE BALLPARK, SO UNBELIEVABLY NEAR IT --

YOUNG KEVIN.

YOU SMELL IT...

KEVIN'S DAD.

AND TASTE IT...

BOTH.

AND CHEER IT...

KEVIN'S DAD.

THE SEATS WHERE THE MAYOR SITS WITH HOLLYWOOD STARS –

THE BIGSHOTS WITH CHAUFFEURS AND CARS –

YOUNG KEVIN.

AND THIS TIME

YOUNG KEVIN & HIS DAD.

THIS *ONE* TIME –

GROWN KEVIN, YOUNG KEVIN & HIS DAD.

THEY'RE OURS.

*(***YOUNG KEVIN** *and his* **DAD** *exit.)*

GROWN KEVIN. *(In the subway car.)* And so it's the day before the game and I can't wait for my Dad to get home. Except as soon as he comes through the door, I can see something's wrong. Mr. Winston, he says, he forgot he promised me the tickets and he gave them to some client or some cousin, so I'm sorry, but we're not going. Well, I guess I cried a little and my Mom put me to bed, but before I know it somebody's shaking me awake and it's my Dad.

Young Kevin's Apartment

(**YOUNG KEVIN** *enters with his* **DAD**.)

YOUNG KEVIN. Dad, what's going on?

KEVIN'S DAD.
TO HELL WITH MISTER WINSTON!
I EARN AN HONEST LIVIN'.
MY MONEY'S GOOD AS HIS IS!

YOUNG KEVIN & HIS DAD.
WE'RE GOIN' TO THE GAME!

(The subway doors open. Bleacher benches are pulled out. **GROWN KEVIN** *goes through the doors and joins* **YOUNG KEVIN** *and his* **DAD**, *heading towards the.)*

Polo Grounds Ticket Window

CONCESSION SALESMAN. Beer here! Getcha your cold beer! Popcorn! Peanuts! Cracker Jack!

MIGUEL.	**ZACK.**	**NEIL.**	**CINDY.**
Jesus, what...?	It's the Polo Grounds.	Ohmigod...	Neil...

> (**KEVIN'S DAD** *buys a beer and a couple of hot dogs.*)

TICKET SELLER. Ten minutes to "play ball!"

KEVIN'S DAD. *(To* **YOUNG KEVIN.***)*
> WE'LL GET THE V.I.P. SEATS.
> THEY COST A PRETTY PENNY.

GROWN KEVIN.
> EXCEPT THERE WEREN'T ANY.
> IT WAS LATE WHEN WE CAME.

KEVIN'S DAD.
> I MADE MY KID A PROMISE: A PAIR BEHIND THE DUGOUT.

TICKET SELLER.
> I ONLY GOT DE BLEACHERS.
> PAY UP, PAL, OR GET'CHER MUG OUT.

> (**YOUNG KEVIN** *and his* **DAD** *climb up into –.*)

The Polo Ground Bleachers

GROWN KEVIN.
AND SO WE TOOK THE BLEACHERS.

KEVIN'S DAD.
BEATS THE RADIO.

YOUNG KEVIN. *(Faking enthusiasm.)*
A LOT...

> (**KEVIN'S DAD** *squints, trying to see the distant baseball diamond.*)

KEVIN'S DAD.
YOU GET THE PANORAMA...

GROWN KEVIN.
LIKE ANTARCTICA BUT HOT...

ALL THREE.
WE GOT...THE WORST SEATS IN THE BALLPARK!

GROWN KEVIN.
THE CLOUDS OF UPPER MANHATTAN.

YOUNG KEVIN. *(Straining to see.)*
WHO'S PITCHIN'?

KEVIN'S DAD. *(Blinded by the sun.)*
WHO'S BATTIN'?

GROWN KEVIN.
MY PRETZEL IS SOGGY.

KEVIN'S DAD.
MY HOT DOG IS COLD.

GROWN KEVIN.
MY PEANUTS ARE MOLDY.

YOUNG KEVIN.
MY CRACKERJACKS ARE OLD.

GROWN KEVIN.

WE'RE LIKE A MILE AND A HALF FROM THE INFIELD.

KEVIN'S DAD. *(Despondent.)*

WHERE SCHMOS LIKE DOORMEN GET SEATED.

GROWN KEVIN.

HE SOUNDED COMPLETELY...DEFEATED.

KEVIN'S DAD. *(To* **YOUNG KEVIN,** *bleakly.)*

YOU'D HEAR MORE AT HOME ON THE RADIO SHOW.

GROWN KEVIN.

IT SCARED ME TO SEE HIM SO LOW...

YOUNG KEVIN.

LET'S STAY, POP.

>   *(Reluctantly.)*

WELL, MAYBE...

>   *(***KEVIN'S DAD** *stands to leave, motions for* **YOUNG KEVIN** *to get up.)*

KEVIN'S DAD.

LET'S GO.

>   *(We hear the crack of the bat, the slightly tinny sound of the* **CROWD** *as if heard through a radio in 1954.)*

GROWN KEVIN. And it's at that exact moment that Vic Wertz, the Indians first basemen, hits this enormous line drive to straight away center field.

KEVIN'S DAD. Ah, *Wertz!*

>   *(Overlapping is the voice of* **RUSS HODGES,** *the Giants' play-by-play announcer.)*

HODGES. *(Voice over.)* There's a long drive, way back in center field...Way back, back, it's...

GROWN KEVIN.
> OF COURSE I CAN'T QUITE SEE IT
> 'CAUSE WERTZ IS LIKE AN ANT,
> BUT FIFTY-THOUSAND PEOPLE
> GO HYSTERICAL AND CHANT.
> I TURN BACK TO THE OUTFIELD,
> AND WHAT IS IT I SEE?

YOUNG KEVIN & GROWN KEVIN.
> WILLIE MAYS IS RUNNING AND –
> ...HE'S COMING STRAIGHT AT ME!

HODGES. *(Voice-over.)* Oh my Lord...!

> *(Time is suspended. The ball is sailing, in slow-motion, directly towards* **YOUNG KEVIN**.*)*

> *(He looks up at the ball, then down at the field, as* **WILLIE MAYS** *appears, in slow motion, reaching out for the ball with his back to the audience and to home plate.)*

GROWN KEVIN.
> I FEEL LIKE I'M THE BULLSEYE.
> THE ARROW IS THE BALL,
> OR EVEN MORE A *METEOR*
> 'CUZ NOW IT AIN'T SO SMALL...

HODGES. *(Echoing distantly.)* Oh my Lord...!

GROWN KEVIN.
> IT'S HURTLING LIKE A COMET...!
> IT'S ALMOST IN MY LAP...!
> THEN WILLIE HOLDS HIS GLOVE OUT,
> AND I SEE BENEATH HIS CAP...

> *(***WILLIE MAYS**, *looking up to get a bead on the ball, locks eyes with* **YOUNG KEVIN** *for a moment.)*

GROWN KEVIN.
...AND AS HIS EYES SWEEP UP,
I SWEAR THEY LOCK ON MINE.
HE SHOOTS ME HIS WORLD-FAMOUS GRIN...
AND AS HE MAKES THE CATCH
THAT TURNED WATER INTO WINE,
HE WINKS AT ME AS IF TO SAY:
"THEM CRUMMY SEATS YOU'RE IN...?
NOW THEY'RE THE BEST...!"

(In slow motion, **WILLIE** *makes "the catch,"
then the action returns to real time.)*

YOUNG KEVIN & GROWN KEVIN.
SO CLOSE YOU ALMOST CAN FEEL IT...

*(***KEVIN'S DAD*** slips his arm around* **YOUNG
KEVIN***'s shoulder.)*

KEVIN'S DAD.
AND SEE IT...

GROWN KEVIN.
AND HEAR IT...

YOUNG KEVIN.
THE CATCH OF THE
BALLGAME.

KEVIN'S DAD.
(Awestruck.)
THE CATCH OF THE *YEAR.*

HODGES.
(Voice-over.) Oh my Lord,
it's hauled in by Willie
Mays! Willie Mays just
brought this crowd to it's
feet, with a catch which
must have been an optical
illusion...!

GROWN KEVIN.
WHEN BASEBALL WAS BASEBALL,
AND EVERYTHING WAS CLEAR...
I HAD THE BEST GODDAMN SEATS IN THE BALLPARK.
AND NOW, I'LL HAVE THEM FOREVER.

KEVIN'S DAD.
   THE MOMENT TO GIVE UP...IS NEVER.

    *(***YOUNG KEVIN** *hugs his* **DAD.***)*

GROWN KEVIN. *(Joining his* **DAD** *and his younger self.)*
   THE CROWD GOIN' CRAZY,
   MY NINE-YEAR-OLD GLEE.
   MY FATHER, AS PROUD AS CAN BE,
   FOREVER WITH WILLIE...AND ME.

    (And as the **CROWD** *roar hits a climax,*
    KEVIN, *his* **DAD,** *and his younger self*
    disappear into eternity and the subway doors
    slide closed... A beat, then **MIGUEL** *drops to*
    his knees.)

MIGUEL. ¡Padre Dios, Santa María y Espíritu Santo! ¡Que
dios bendiga! In the name of Jesus, Amen!

   (He crosses himself furiously.)

NEIL. It isn't fair. This is not fair –

CINDY. Honey –

NEIL. *No.* This is a *cheat.* I put everything on hold. My
whole life. In high school so I'd get into the right
college. In college so I'd get into the right med school.
In med school I'd get the right internship. And now,
when I'm almost done – when *we're* almost done – we
walk into a broken elevator and that's it?!

STANLEY. It happens when it happens.

ZACK. "It happens when it happens." That's deep, man.

NEIL. Not fair...

GINA. Putting things off, I was never any good at that –

MAURICE. Hornyhardhats.com. That's what was up on my
computer screen when I left the apartment.

ARLENE. I was supposed to see my therapist this afternoon. I was going to tell her she'd wasted ten years of my life, then flip her over backwards in her Barcelona chair.

CINDY. I had an argument with my mom last night. I told her to stay out of my life and slammed down the phone.

GINA. When I was eight my mom took me to the beauty parlor with her and I saw my first copy of *Vogue*. Maybe I'm just shallow and self-absorbed, but there was a photo spread inside – a New Year's Eve party at a palazzo on the Grand Canal – and I knew that was the life I had to have and I just went for it.

CINDY. I think maybe you're right...maybe you are just shallow and self-absorbed.

GINA. You know, I'm sorry you lived a dead-end life –

MIGUEL. *(Rolling over her, to* **STANLEY**.*)* Yo, yo, Stanley. My man. I left a lot of stuff undone. Good deeds, shit like that. So if there was any way –

> *(He gives* **STANLEY** *the "Headwaiter's Handshake."* **STANLEY** *holds up a twenty-dollar bill.)*

STANLEY. Really?

> *(To everyone.)*

What's done is done. I coulda this, I shoulda that – it's all a waste of time. Think about what *was*, like Helen did, and Kevin did.

ZACK. And me? Is that what I should be doing, Stanley? Thinking about what was?

STANLEY. I don't know what you're talking about.

ZACK. Oh, yes, you do. Because I *do* remember waiting on the platform. I *do* remember shoving my way onto this train. These people may all be dead and that's really weird and I'm sorry. But I'm not dead, and I don't belong here.

STANLEY. I'm aware of that.

ZACK. He's "aware" of it.

STANLEY. I get a manifest –

(*Indicating his clipboard.*)

This one's got eight names on it. Hathaway, Maurice. Slater, Arlene.

ZACK. But no Zacks.

STANLEY. No Zacks. You're definitely not supposed to be here. Zack.

ZACK. Then what exactly am I doing here?

STANLEY. Well, I'm just guessing, but I'll bet you were probably in such a hard-charger hurry to get yourself someplace else that you took a wrong turn and bulled your way into someplace where you don't belong.

ZACK. Fine. Let's decide that that's what happened. Let's stipulate to that. The important point is we both agree that this subway car is not where I'm supposed to be. So how 'bout if you just wave your magic Metro Card, or whatever it is you do, and send me back?

NEIL. Wait a minute, you mean he gets to go back?

MIGUEL. Not without me, baby!

ARLENE. Or me!

STANLEY. (*Firmly.*) He's not going anywhere.

ZACK. You just said I don't belong here.

STANLEY. No. But here you are. You put yourself here. And here's where you're gonna stay.

ZACK. And who decides that? *You*? Some low-level loser bureaucrat gets to make decisions about life and death? I don't think so. You know, I never thought much about what happens when you die –

STANLEY. *(Cutting him off.)* Or about much of anything except your next million dollar verdict. But listen to me. No one – no one's ever been sent back. It's never happened and it's never going to. And if it ever did, I can promise you some self-involved "master-of-the-universe-in-training" who thinks life is all about making partner at *Paul, Weiss* is not gonna be the first!

GINA. *(To* **STANLEY.***)* Excuse me, could I ask you something –?

STANLEY. *(Sharply.)* What?

GINA. I just want to make sure I understand the rules. I pick a moment, the way Helen did, the way Kevin did, and then those doors open and I disappear into that moment forever and ever, is that right?

STANLEY. That's right. So you want to make sure –

[MUSIC NO. 6 "GSTAAD"]

GINA.

GSTAAD.

STANLEY. Gstaad?

GINA.

I CHOOSE GSTAAD.
WE'D BEEN SKIING
AND MY ANKLE, IT GOT TWISTED.
WHILE THE STAFF MASSAGED MY FEET,
WE HAD DINNER IN OUR SUITE.
THE WAITER BROUGHT CRISTAL,
FRANÇOIS INSISTED.

CINDY. Who?

GINA.

TWO-THOUSAND-TWO...
THE SLOPES WERE BRIGHT WITH SNOW.
THE VIEW OF LAKE GENEVA, A POSTCARD.

MAURICE. Oh?

GINA.

> AND WHEN THE MOON
> ROSE OVER THE MATTERHORN,
> I REMEMBER FEELIN' KINDA
> LIKE I'D DIED AND BEEN REBORN...
> ...IN GSTAAD
> WITH *CHER* FRANÇOIS,
> EYES AGLITTER LIKE OUR FLUTES OF BACCARAT.
>
> IF I COULD CHOOSE ONE MOMENT,
> ONE PEFECT MAN,
> IT'S GSTAAD.
> AND NOW GUESS WHAT? I CAN!

MAURICE. Yes, darling, well, *perhaps* you can.

GINA. Of course I can. You heard him –

MAURICE. You say the moon came up over the Matterhorn?

GINA. Like a big scoop of Breyer's vanilla ice cream, with flecks.

MAURICE. Darling, the Matterhorn's in Zermatt, not Gstaad.

GINA. In *Zermatt*? Are you...? Why, of course it is! In the moonlight I guess all those Alps sort of look alike!

MAURICE. They may. But none of them looks like a lake.

GINA. A *lake*?

MAURICE. I spent Christmas in Gstaad last year with the Agnelli's, and the closest we got to a view of Lake Geneva was a scenic photo on a beer coaster.

GINA. All right, you know what? Auf wiedersehen, Gstaad, I've got a better moment anyway!

STANLEY. I'm sure you do, but maybe –

GINA.

> SOUTH BEACH.
> SO CHI-CHI *RICHE*.

WHERE ALL HOLLYWOOD
AND FASHION LETS ITS HAIR DOWN.
AT THE DELANO, NO LESS.

    (To **MAURICE.***)*

WELL, YOU'VE HEARD OF IT?

MAURICE. *(Spoken in rhythm.)*
OOHH, YES.

GINA.
COMPARED TO IT
THE EDEN ROC'S A TEAR-DOWN.

MIGUEL. Hey, I got a cousin parks cars at the Eden Roc –

GINA.
TWO-THOUSAND-THREE...
THE BATHROOM HAD A SPA.
AMENITIES BY ACQUA DI PARMA.
AND BEST OF ALL
JAMAL PLANNED A BIG SURPRISE.
DOWN THE STAIRCASE TO THE ROSE BAR
WHO IS THERE BEFORE MY EYES?
JUDE LAW!

MIGUEL. Who?

GINA.
I'M LIKE, IN AWE!
WITH THE BLUEST PAIR OF EYES I EVER SAW.
WITH CHILLED CRISTAL,
JUDE LAW AND THE OCEAN VIEWS,
KEEP GSTAAD.
IT'S MIAMI I CHOOSE.

MAURICE. Jude Law. That's quite a moment, darling, I almost can't believe it.

GINA. Believe me, I couldn't either.

MAURICE. No, I mean I almost can't believe it, because I don't think it could have happened.

GINA. Couldn't have happened? I was *there*!

MAURICE. Are you sure?

GINA. Of course I'm sure!

MAURICE. Because The Rose Bar was closed almost all of two thousand and three while it was being redecorated top to bottom – by yours truly.

STANLEY. O.K., time out here –

GINA. *(Defiantly.)*
CANNES!
FILM FESTIVAL,
TWO-THOUSAND-FOUR.
ALL THAT EURO-YADA-YADA,
I WAS THERE AN' WEARIN' PRADA
WHEN I HAD A RENDEZVOUS –

ARLENE.
SHE'S IMAGINING IT ALL.

GINA.
WITH THE PRINCE OF MONTENEGRO –

NEIL.
SHE'S COMPLETELY OFF THE WALL.

GINA. *(Triumphantly.)*
IN A ROLLS...EQUIPPED WITH CHILLED CRISTAL!

PASSENGERS. *(Variously, overlapping.)* Does *any* of this make sense?...Not a lot...Talk about over the top –

STANLEY. Listen, Gina, I'm really going to insist you give yourself a little bit more time –

GINA. I don't need a little bit more time!

> *(A burst of inspiration, a place to top them all.)*

DUBAI! I'VE DONE DUBAI!

CINDY.
WHAT, YOU GOOGLED IT ON GOOGLE? SO HAVE I!

GINA. *(Sharply, to* **CINDY.***)*
AND WHO PUT YOU IN CHARGE OF THE FIRING
SQUAD? SCRATCH DUBAI! I'VE DECIDED –
GSTAAD!

STANLEY. You know, Gina, there's a way that this works
and a way that it doesn't, so you have to make sure that
the moment you choose –

(She steps assertively up to the sliding doors.)

GINA.
OKAY, DOORS! OPEN WIDE.
HERE'S MY CHANCE OF A LIFETIME – NOW *SLIDE!*

(Nothing happens.)

SUMPIN'S OFF...SUMPIN'S ODD...

(Peers through the glass, pounds the door.)

WHERE'S THE SNOW?
LET ME GO!
OHMIGOD...
WHERE'S GSTAAD?

*(A beat. She sags, slides down with her back
against the unopened doors.)*

MAURICE. *(Offering her a hand.)* Gina...Gina, darling –

GINA. *(Refusing it.)* You know, I think I was a little too
polite with you, Maurice. I think maybe I should have
just told you to mind your own business.

MAURICE. I'm sorry, darling, but –

GINA. Just told you to shut the hell up and mind your
own business. "The Rose Bar was being redecorated."
"I spent Christmas with the Agnellis in Gstaad."

STANLEY. Gina –

GINA. Well, you want to know where *I* spent Christmas, Maurice? This year? Last year? Behind the *Chanel* counter at *Bloomingdale's*. You know that salesgirl who tries to spray you with some new cologne you don't want to buy? You ever wonder what her story is? What her dreams were when she was just a kid? Well, they weren't about selling perfume at a department store, Maurice. No. My dream was to be part of a glittering, glamorous world I'd seen in a glossy magazine when I was eight years old. So when I turned eighteen and my parents couldn't stop me anymore, I moved to Manhattan. Where I knocked on doors from *Wilhelmina* to *Eileen Ford* until my money ran out and I took what I told myself was a seasonal sales job at *Bloomingdale's*...Where now I am a fixture, Maurice. There I stand, day in, day out. Smile and spray. Smile and spray...And pretty soon I start to daydream. Where's that classy couple going for dinner? Where's that fashionable man going on vacation? And before too long those day dream lives start to seem real – realer than the dead-end life I'm living – and I think maybe I'm going crazy, but I'd rather go crazy than go back home. And then, today, a miracle. I get killed in a construction accident and suddenly in death I see a chance to have what I could never have in life. So I design my moment – full of glamour and romance and champagne – but stupid me, I put the Matterhorn in the wrong place and the next thing I know some smug celebrity designer has reached out and snatched it all back. Well, what did I expect? What made me think a stupid, smile-and-spray shop girl would be welcome in your world, even after I was dead?

CINDY. Gina, I'm sorry...

MAURICE. Darling –

GINA. *(Deliberately mispronouncing his name.)* Fuck you, Mau-reece.

STANLEY. Listen, Gina, you can blame Maurice if you want to, but it was never going to work –

GINA. No, nothing ever does, does it?

ZACK. He means because the moment that you pick has to be *real*, right?

GINA. Real. Like the fabulous *Chanel* counter, that kind of real?

STANLEY. There's only one kind of real, Gina. What is. What was.

MAURICE. Gina, listen. Dubai, South Beach. That life…it's not the life you think it is.

GINA. Oh, I know. It's empty, hollow. Which is why it's the life *you* chose.

MAURICE. Because it was the *work* I did. But if I was ready to choose my moment – and I suppose I've been ready for the last twenty years – it wouldn't have anything to do with champagne or Gstaad.

[MUSIC NO. 6A "HOSPITAL CUE"]

A Hospital Room, Mount Sinai Hospital

*(The subway doors open onto a private room overlooking Central Park. In a hospital bed is **ALBERT**. It's 1988. A nurse, **HYACINTH**, is helping **ALBERT** back into bed and pulling the covers up around him...)*

HYACINTH. There now, honey, doesn't that feel better? All bathed and freshened up?

ALBERT. What time is it? Is it three o'clock?

HYACINTH. Don't worry, honey. He'll be here. That gentleman of yours hasn't missed an afternoon yet.

*(**MAURICE** steps out of the shadows carrying a designer tote bag and a shopping bag from Zabar's.)*

MAURICE. Hello, Albert.

ALBERT. Hello, Maurice.

MAURICE. Hello, Hyacinth.

HYACINTH. Oh, hello honey. Lord am I glad to see you. Do you mind keeping an eye on this one for a minute? I worked right through my break and I need to run out and make a purchase.

MAURICE. *(Taking a dollar out of his pocket.)* Well, then, make a purchase for me, too, all right? I wrote my numbers on Washington's wig.

HYACINTH. *(To **ALBERT**.)* Honey, I don't know what you are doing with this incorrigible man.

*(Takes dollar, to **MAURICE**.)*

Nothing in that bag that's not permitted in this room, is there?

MAURICE. I know the rules, darling.

HYACINTH. *(Handing him a surgical mask.)* Won't be a minute...

MAURICE. Take your time...

*(She leaves. **MAURICE** wanders to the window.)*

Mrs. Vanden Heuval may take the prize for 1988's most insufferable client, but she certainly got you a room with a view.

ALBERT. And I'm sure you thanked her for me –

*(As **MAURICE** starts to slip on the mask.)*

Don't bother putting the mask on.

MAURICE. Why not?

ALBERT. Because we both know I'm not coming home this time, Maurice.

MAURICE. I brought you something.

ALBERT. Did you? Thank you.

MAURICE. You remember last July? The *Philharmonic in the Park* and the *Cheese Lovers Picnic Basket* from *Zabar's*? Well I thought, we've got the Park, what if we had the blanket –

(He takes one out of the tote bag.)

And the Mahler –

(He takes a boombox out of the tote bag.)

And the –

ALBERT. Stop it, Maurice. For God's sake, stop! Just sit, all right? Sit over there. Read a book or watch TV. I don't want to be cheered up. And I certainly don't want to have a picnic.

MAURICE. Well then, we won't.

> (*A beat. He glances out the window at the park.*)

[MUSIC NO. 7 "THE BOY INSIDE YOUR EYES"]

The leaves are changing...
YOU AND I
SEEM LIKE STRANGERS
RUNNING OUT OF THINGS TO SAY.
READ A BOOK.
WATCH A GAME SHOW
AS WE PASS THE TIME OF DAY,
ACROSS THE ROOM
A MILLION MILES AWAY...
...AND THEN,
THE BOY INSIDE YOUR EYES
LOOKS UP AT ME AND SMILES,
AND I REMEMBER WHO YOU USED TO BE.
FOR WHEN
I LOOK INSIDE YOUR EYES
I SEE...
SOMEONE STRONG.
FULL OF CONFIDENCE.
THINKING BIG AND MOVING FAST.
WHAT WENT WRONG?
WAS IT BOTH OF US?
CAN WE FIND OUR WAY BACK HOME,
OR HAS THE MOMENT PASSED?

ALBERT. The moment? What's the moment that you want, Maurice?

MAURICE. All of them. Any of them. This one.

ALBERT. This one? This one is not how I want to be remembered.

MAURICE. *(Sits beside him on the bed.)* Believe it or not this moment...is not the only moment I see when I look at you.

THE NIGHT ON FIRE ISLAND
THAT DRIFTED INTO DAY.
THE FERRY BOAT TO FAIRY BLISS
ACROSS THE GREAT SOUTH BAY.
CENTRAL PARK, ON THE MORNING
OF THE AFTER-CHRISTMAS SALES,
WHEN WE TREKKED THROUGH A BLIZZARD

> *(**ALBERT** starts to soften.)*

ALBERT & MAURICE.

ALL THE WAY TO BLOOMINGDALE'S...

MAURICE.

RELATIONSHIPS LIKE HOME DÉCOR
ARE ALL IN SMALL DETAILS...

Well...

> *(**MAURICE** offers **ALBERT** a cracker. **ALBERT** makes a face.)*

They're salt-free. Try *one.*

ALBERT. All right, already. One.

> *(He takes the cracker, takes a bite.)*

MAURICE. Good?

ALBERT. Good.

MAURICE.

PEOPLE CHANGE
THROUGH THE SEASONS.
LIKE NEW YORK,
THE PASSING SHOW...

MAURICE.
LITTLE LIES,
BURIED SECRETS
EVERYBODY HAS, I KNOW.
YOU THINK YOU'VE LOST
THAT SPARK OF LONG AGO...

ALBERT. *(Sitting up in bed.)* No.

      *(***MAURICE*** turns.)*

No.

MAURICE.
...AND THEN
THE BOY INSIDE YOUR EYES
LOOKS UP AT ME AND SMILES,
AND I REMEMBER WHO *I* USED TO BE.
FOR WHEN
YOU LOOK INSIDE MY EYES
YOU SEE
ALL MY HOPE.
ALL MY HAPPINESS.
MOMENTS ETCHED IN MEMORY...

      *(Over underscore, ***ALBERT*** slips a ring off his finger and slips it on ***MAURICE****'s finger.)*

...AND I TAKE YOU, AS YOU TAKE ME.

[MUSIC 7A – AFTER "THE BOY INSIDE YOUR EYES"]

      *(***ALBERT*** breaks the rest of his cracker in half and gives half to ***MAURICE***. They share the cracker and clasp hands...as the doors to the subway close and they disappear. A long beat of stillness and silence.)*

MIGUEL. My man Mo. I'm sorry he died.

NEIL. I'm sorry we all died.

MIGUEL. Amen to that.

GINA. I never had a moment like that. So simple, and so honest. Or if I did, I don't remember it.

ZACK. A moment like that? How could you forget it?

ARLENE. Two men in bed eating crackers? Easy.

ZACK. Jesus, Arlene, what's wrong with you? Where's your *empathy*?

ARLENE. My empathy? Not all behavior deserves empathy. There's *right* and there's *wrong*. And making moral judgments isn't some kind of hobby, like racquetball, it's an obligation.

MIGUEL. Unbelievable. This chick actually makes my ex-wife sound like Mother Theresa.

ARLENE. Show me your green card.

MIGUEL. My what?

ARLENE. Show me your green card!

STANLEY. Listen, I hate to break this up, all this squabbling is actually pretty entertaining, but I need to remind you, you all have a job to do. You each have a moment to pick.

[MUSIC NO. 8 - "PERFECT MOMENTS"]

NEIL. One single moment. Where do you begin?

CINDY.
    HAVE THEY STARTED MISSING ME, I WONDER?

GINA.
    WHO WILL SPRAY THE PERFUME AT THE STORE?

MIGUEL.
    DOES THIS MEAN I CAN'T GET BLOW JOBS ANYMORE?

ARLENE.

> WHEN THEY LAY ME OUT AT FRANK E. CAMPBELL,
> WILL PEOPLE BE WEEPY-EYED,
> OR SHOW UP TO ASSURE THEMSELVES I DIED?

ZACK.

> PERFECT MOMENTS THAT PASS UNNOTICED.
> PRECIOUS MOMENTS YOU LEAVE UNDONE.

CINDY.

> WHO WILL MAKE THE CHAROSET?

NEIL.

> MRS. GILMAN'S PROGNOSES.

ARLENE & GINA.

> MARATHONS YOU WERE GONNA RUN.

MIGUEL.

> CROSSIN' OVER THE HARLEM RIVER
> LOOKIN' UP AT THE CITY'S GLOW...

ALL. (*Except* **ZACK.**)

> PERFECT MOMENTS,
> I WONDER WHERE THEY GO?

STANLEY. Life goes on, that's the way it works. No one remembers anyone forever. So pick your moments and forget about it, same as they'll forget about you.

ZACK.

> IF I WATCHED MY LIFE ON INSTANT REPLAY,
> LOOKED BACK AT THE DAILY GRIND,
> AND RANKED IT ON A SCALE OF ONE TO TEN...
> WOULD I TAKE THE TIME TO FIND THE MOMENTS
> THESE OTHER NEW YORKERS FIND,
> OR DROP THE BALL AND MISS THEM ALL AGAIN?

ALL.

> PERFECT MOMENTS THAT
> PASS UNNOTICED,

ZACK.

ALL THE WASTED

TILL THE MOMENT YOU   TIME
PASS AWAY.

CINDY.

BARTLETT PEARS AT BALDUCCI'S.

NEIL.

BACON BURGERS WITH BLUE CHEESE.

GINA.

FRESH CANNOLI ON MOTHER'S DAY.

ZACK.   **ALL.**

PERFECT MOMENTS I NEVER PAUSED FOR
IN THE MOMENT THEY PASSED ME BY.   AH...
DO THEY VANISH LIKE CINDERS IN THE SKY?
ALL THE MOMENTS I WONDER...WHERE WAS
   I?
WHERE WAS I?

SOME.

HAVE THEY STARTED MISSING ME, I WONDER.

ZACK.

WHERE WAS I?

ALL.

HAVE THEY STARTED MISSING ME, I WONDER.

ZACK. *(To* **STANLEY.***)* I gotta get out of here!

STANLEY. *(Wearily.)* I thought we'd been *over* this –

ZACK. I gotta go back!

STANLEY. Fine –

    (Offering him the crowbar.)

Give it another shot. I think Neil took a whack at all the
windows, but maybe you'll get luck–

ZACK. I'm asking for your help, Goddamnit! Why won't you help me?!

STANLEY. Because I'm here to help *them*, not *you*.

ZACK. Because they're dead and I'm not.

STANLEY. There you go, Counselor! You see, it's not that complicated.

ZACK. *(Gathering his thoughts.)* No, actually, I guess it's not. They're dead, I'm not. Case closed.

STANLEY. Case closed.

ZACK. Now what about you?

STANLEY. Me?

ZACK. You.

STANLEY. I don't know what you're talking about.

NEIL. I do.

ARLENE. So do I.

ZACK. They're dead. I'm alive. Which one are you?

> *(Ad-libs from* **PASSENGERS***: What about that?!...Which one are you?!...Etc.)*

MIGUEL. Oh, Jesus, he's a *zombie*!

STANLEY. *Listen*. There's nothing about me that's going to change anything for anybody on this train, all right? You each have a job to do. Do it and don't screw it up.

ZACK. Is that what you did, Stanley? Screw it up?

STANLEY. Screw what up?

ZACK. I don't know. Your life, your death. I mean, here you are. And it's unlikely that you dropped dead and that the perfect moment that you picked was one where you rode around the subway system helping dead people pick their perfect moments.

(Derisive laughter from everyone but **STANLEY**.*)*

Fill us in, Stanley. We want to hear *your* story.

(The **PASSENGERS** *pile on, all at once.)*

MIGUEL. *(Simultaneously.)* What about that, man? You're like the king of attitude when it comes to us. How 'bout you tell us a thing or two about *you*?

ARLENE. *(Simultaneously.)* Yes, we do, Stanley. We've been patronized and belittled by you since you showed up with your damned clipboard. Who the hell *are* you?

CINDY. *(Simultaneously.)* He's right, we do. You know everything about *us*. "You walked into an elevator!" What about you? What did you walk in to?

GINA. *(Simultaneously.)* We're supposed to be choosing moments! That's what you told us! But what did *you* choose?! *Did* you choose?! What are you doing here?!

NEIL. *(Simultaneously.)* Zack's right. You made a big speech about what we're doing here and what our "job" is. What about *your* job? What's *your* job, Stanley?

STANLEY. *(Cutting them all off.)* What you want to do is pick your moments and get the hell off this train.

GINA. But what if I can't? What if I never had a moment, or I can't remember one? What do I pick then?!

ZACK. What about that, Stanley?

(Another explosion. Everybody talks at once.)

NEIL. Your job is to help us! Do your job!

ARLENE. *(Simultaneously.)* Answer her question! That's what you're supposed to do!

CINDY. *(Simultaneously.)* Is that it?! Is there some other way to get out of here?!

GINA. *(Simultaneously.)* We need help! You're supposed to be *helping* us!

ZACK. *(Simultaneously, cheerfully.)* The act was going great, Stanley. It's not going so great now, is it?

MIGUEL. *(Overlapping.)* No justice, no peace! No justice, no peace! No justice, no peace! No justice, no –!

STANLEY. *(Cutting them off.) All right*, all right!

    (To **GINA**.*)*

You want to know what happens if you can't pick? Listen up –

    (To **ZACK**.*)*

And you, Clarence Darrow. You wanted to know Stanley's story? Pay attention...

    (To all the **PASSENGERS**.*)*

I died in 1986 at the age of forty-two of a massive coronary. It happened in a private dining room at the 21 Club. I was an investment banker. A master of the leveraged buyout. The great big bad Barbarian at the Gate.

[MUSIC NO. 9 "STEP UP THE LADDER"]

I had just engineered a hostile take-over of a tire company in Ohio which had made the four other men in that dining room wealthy beyond their wildest dreams. And they were saying...

    (Shadowy figures appear: the **SUITS**, *businessmen – drinking whisky, standing in abstract Citizen Kane-ish slashes of light.)*

SUITS.
  THANK YOU! THANK YOU!
  THANK YOU, YOU SON OF A BITCH!

TONIGHT WE SALUTE YOU
FOR MAKIN' US RICH!

STANLEY.
"FRIENDS, I COULDN'T HAVE
DONE IT ALONE," I REPLY.
"TO THAT TRIO OF TEAMWORK:
ME, MYSELF, AND I!"

SUITS.
HA-HA-HA.
HA-HA-HA.
HA-HA-HA-HA-HA-HA-HA-HA-HA-HA.
HERE'S TO THAT...EAGER BEAVER
OF CORPORATE RAIDING!

STANLEY.
YOUR OVER-ACHIEVER
OF INSIDER-TRADING!

SUITS.
TAKE A STEP UP THE LADDER

STANLEY.
A DEAL AT A TIME!

SUITS.
A STEP UP THE LADDER

STANLEY.
OF LEGALIZED CRIME!

SUITS.
CHEERS TO OUR...WALL STREET BUDDHA,
HIS MANTRA OF MANNA!

STANLEY.
THE TOP BARRACUDA!
THE PARK AVE PIRANHA!

SUITS. *(Now puffing Cuban cigars, bringing on a ladder.)*
TAKE A STEP UP THE LADDER,
THE LIMIT'S THE SKY!

STANLEY.
JUST FOLLOW MY MOTTO – I LIE!

>   (**STANLEY** *climbs the ladder, magically escaping from the subway car...*)

STANLEY.
HERE'S TO THE JAG!
FORMAL DRAG
BY MY PERSONAL FAG!
AND THE CHOPPER
TO MY PROPERTY IN QUOGUE!
HERE'S TO THE "DON'T-LOOK"
BLUE-BOOK
CHARITABLE CAUSES
THAT ANNOINTED A PRINCE FROM A FROG!
HERE'S TO THE PUNY MINNOWS
FREE-ENTERPRISE WINNOWS
WHILE SHYSTERS LIKE US SLICE THE PIE!

SUITS.
AY! AY! AY!

STANLEY.
TAKE A STEP UP THE LADDER!
WHOEVER I STEP ON,
CAN JUST KISS MY *TUCHAS* AND DIE!

ARLENE. Charming.

STANLEY. Talking Straighter to Arlene Slater!

>   (*A grin, back to the* **PASSENGERS**.*)*

'Cause that's how it happened in the Eighties, folks. Hot times for guys like me, right, Zack? Zack knows. Hell, he probably studied some of the deals I put together in business school.

ZACK. Law school.

STANLEY. Whatever. The thing is, if greed was good, my life was *great*.

THE TROPHY WIFE
CHEATING LIFE
WITH A SURGICAL KNIFE!
KITCHEN MAKE-OVERS
MY TAKE-OVERS PROVIDE!
HERE'S TO THE COKED-UP
D-CUP
WOULD-BE-ACTRESS MODEL
WHO I CODDLE IN 'LUDES ON THE SIDE!
HERE'S TO THE...
KOONS AND SCHNABELS
PROSPERITY GOBBLES!
THE STUDIO 54 HIGH!

> *(As the* **SUITS** *sing,* **STANLEY** *climbs the ladder again, ultimately perching on the top.)*

SUITS.

AY! AY! AY!
AY! AY! AY!
AY! AY! AY!
OY! OY! OY!

STANLEY. *(Grips his heart.)*

BUT THEN A STEP UP THE LADDER,
A PAIN IN MY CHEST
KNOCKS ME FLAT
IN MY PÂTÉ DE MUSCOVY BREAST!
MY "SALUTE"
WAS ACUTE CORONARY ARREST.
IN MY SCHLELP UP THE LADDER, I DIE!
KISS MY GOLD-PLATED TUCHAS BYE-BYE.

> *(Post-mortem,* **STANLEY** *finds himself in a way-station to death, not unlike the subway car...only it's not a subway.)*

STANLEY. When I come to I'm in this totally other place – the cabin of an American Airlines 737 waiting to take off at O'Hare. And not even business class – coach! But we never take off. All around me are people I have never seen before, all wondering how they got there, until the Stewardess came out and explained the rules.

STEWARDESS. This journey is what comes next. Not always on a plane. Different people make the trip in different ways. But everybody makes it – and everybody gets a chance, one chance, to pick a perfect moment from their lives and to live in the eternal bliss of that moment.

STANLEY. And everybody on that plane bitched and moaned, just like you all did, till finally they settled down and picked their moments...

MAN #1.
A BARBEQUE THE DAY BEFORE I LEFT FOR VIETNAM.

(He vanishes.)

LITTLE GIRL.
THE NUTCRACKER SUITE WITH MY MOM.

(She vanishes.)

STANLEY. And I'm thinking...

MAN #2.
MY WINNING HAND IN VEGAS.

(He vanishes.)

WOMAN #1.
MY FINAL CIGARETTE.

(She vanishes.)

WOMAN #2.
MARIA SINGING "TOSCA" AT THE MET.

*(She vanishes. No one is left but **STANLEY**.)*

STEWARDESS. Stanley? Stanley, did you pick your moment?

STANLEY.
I WRACK MY BRAIN FOR MEMORIES.
NOT ONE DO I RECALL.
'CAUSE NOTHING I HAVE EVER DONE
MEANS ANYTHING AT ALL.
WITHOUT A HAPPY MOMENT,
I SEE TO MY CHAGRIN
I CAN'T GO BACK TO WHERE I'VE NEVER BEEN.

STEWARDESS. If you can't pick, Stanley, or you *won't* pick, you ride.

STANLEY. I "ride?"

STEWARDESS. Some on subway cars, some on elevators, some, like myself, on a plane. That's what those of us with no moments do. We...

(Spoken in rhythm.)

...RIDE AND GUIDE.
RIDE AND GUIDE.
RIDE AND GUIDE.
RIDE AND GUIDE.

(She disappears.)

STANLEY.
AND AS THE...DAYS I SQUANDERED
RECEDE IN THE DISTANCE,
HOW OFTEN I'VE PONDERED
THE JOYS OF EXISTENCE.
WHEN YOU'VE TOTALLY MISSED 'EM,
WITH NOWHERE TO GO,
YOU WORK FOR "THE SYSTEM,"
FOREVER –

GINA. *(Paling, panicky.)*

  (Spoken in rhythm.)
   OH NO...!

STANLEY.
   YOU GET ASSIGNED TO A FERRY,
   A TRAIN OR A BOEING
   WITH PASSENGERS VERY
   DISMAYED TO BE GOING.

   YOU'RE THEIR COSMIC CONDUCTOR
   FROM THIS STOP TO THAT,
   BUT YOU GOTTA STOP WHERE YOU'RE AT.

   AND SO YOU RIDE.
   YOU'RE THE GUIDE
   THERE TO HELP 'EM DECIDE
   ON WHICH HIGHLIGHT
   FROM THE TWILIGHT OF THEIR PAST.
   YET FROM THAT COLD HARD,
   GOLD CARD
   WORLD OF ACQUISITION,
   I'M A MAN WITH A "MISSION" AT LAST...

       (He turns coldly to **ZACK**.*)*

   BUT AS FOR YOU, GO-GETTER,
   YOU DID ME ONE BETTER.
   YOU SHOVED YOUR WAY ON HERE, AND WHY?

ZACK. *By mistake!*

       *(**STANLEY** kicks the subway car and sets it
       spinning.)*

STANLEY.
   FOR THAT STEP UP THE LADDER
   YOU COULD NOT RESIST!
   WITH YOUR EYE ON THE PRIZE
   OF THE PARTNERSHIP LIST!

STANLEY.

WELL, *SCHLEMIEL,*
HERE'S THE DEAL:
YOU JUST SLIT YOUR OWN WRIST!
ONCE THE TRAIN LEAVES THE STATION,
IT'S GONE!
NO ONE EVER WENT BACK
WHO GOT ON!
DON'T COME RUNNING TO ME, PAL, TO CRY.

> (**STANLEY** *has again climbed to the top rung of the ladder.*)

STANLEY & ALBERT.

ONCE YOU STEP OFF THE LADDER ...

STANLEY.

YOU DIE.

> (*He leaps off the ladder and lands back inside the subway car.*)

Now, aren't you glad you asked?

GINA. That's me, what he described. From smile and spray to ride and guide! I'm going to wind up just like that stewardess!

STANLEY. It's certainly a possibility. And not just you. Neil? Cindy? Miguel? How 'bout you, Arlene?

ARLENE. Shut the hell up.

STANLEY. What do *you* think, Zack? You're the guy who cornered the poor witness and –

ZACK. (*Grabbing him.*) You son-of-a-bitch –!

STANLEY. What are you going to do, Zack? Kill me?

ZACK. (*Throwing him aside.*) I'm not going to wind up trapped like you!

STANLEY. Like me? No. But there's only one way off this train. Dead people pick their perfect moments, those doors open, and they go through. But you, Zack, you aren't dead, and even if you were, I don't think you've ever had a perfect moment. So I'd say you're going to be trapped on this train for a very long time – alone. Alone...

ZACK. No!

[MUSIC NO. 9A "ZACK'S RANT"]

ZACK.

IT'S JUST ANOTHER SITUATION!
ANOTHER SET-BACK TO RESOLVE!
THE KIND OF *POSTHOC* LITIGATION
I GET PAID BIG BUCKS TO SOLVE!
NO LITTLE SUBWAY MUSSOLINI
CAN MAKE A DARTMOUTH MAN KOW-TOW!

STANLEY. Ooo!

ZACK.

WHEN I'VE GOTTEN IN SCRAPES,
I KEEP GOIN' THE DISTANCE!
NARROW ESCAPES
ARE MY *PIÈCE DE RÉSISTANCE*!
NINE TIMES IN TEN,
THERE'S A CLAUSE OR A LOOPHOLE!
FIND IT AND THEN,
GET THE HELL OUT OF DODGE, SOMEHOW!

STANLEY. *(Spoken in ryhthm.)*
JUST NOT RIGHT NOW.

ZACK. There's gotta be a precedent. Some exculpatory clause. A writ. Habeas corpus! Think. Think. I'll think of something...

      (**NEIL** *stands abruptly, breathing heavily.*)

CINDY. Neil, are you O.K.?

(*A hiss, to* **STANLEY.**)

Look what you did –

(*Back to* **NEIL,** *quickly.*)

I mean, you *are* O.K., I know that. But just in case you wanted the inhaler –

NEIL. I picked my moment, Cindy.

CINDY. You did?

NEIL. At least I think I did. But before I tell you what it is, I want you to know I understand that you might pick a moment from your life before you met me, or maybe *after* you met me that I wasn't part of. Maybe something with your family, say. And I would understand that. At least I'd try to. Because I know I wasn't always so easy to get along with. And sometimes it must have felt like you had to take care of me. But this moment that I picked...

...at first I thought I shouldn't tell you what it was. But then I thought, no, you should know because you're in it...and I would understand if you didn't *want* to be in it, but –

CINDY. Neil, what's the moment?

NEIL. Do you remember one night about a year after we met? It was really late and the next day was the first day of Chinese New Year and also Tiffany Mandelbaum's Bat Mitzvah –?

(**CINDY** *screams.*)

What is it?! What's the matter?!

CINDY. That's the moment I picked!

NEIL. Come on. The night we stayed up to –?

CINDY. Yes! Yes! I can't believe it!

[MUSIC NO. 9B BEFORE "FLASH CARDS"]

*(They embrace, laughing with a combination of relief and delight, as the subway doors slide open. **NEIL** and **CINDY** pick up their backpacks and walk through the doors into…)*

Neil and Cindy's Apartment

> *(They shed their hospital scrubs, under which they wear their version of pajamas – t-shirts and athletic shorts. They pull a futon-like comforter out of one of the backpacks, two stacks of homemade flashcards, and climb onto the bed.)*

NEIL. Come on, when we did this yesterday, you got four out of...twelve, that's not bad.

[MUSIC NO. 10 "FAMILY FLASHCARDS"]

CINDY. It sucks.

NEIL. It doesn't! You're doing good.

CINDY. Let's take the night off.

NEIL. The night off? Listen, in exactly nine hours you get tossed into the middle of the Mandelbaum Bat Mitzvah and four hours later I sink or swim at the Ch'en family New Year's banquet! This is no time to take the night off.

CINDY. O.K., but after this, it's your turn.

NEIL. Absolutely. Here goes...

> *(Over underscoring, **NEIL** shuffles through the pile of homemade flash cards and aims one at **CINDY**.)*

CINDY. *(Reading.)* "Mezuzah." The thing on the door.

NEIL. What thing on the door? The knob? The knocker?

CINDY. The *thing*. Up there, that you're supposed to rub on your way in.

NEIL. Good.

> *(He reveals the next card.)*

CINDY. "Tzitzit." Uh...

NEIL. Come on, it's a fashion question...

> *(He waves his fingers up and down around his neck.)*

CINDY. The fringes on the prayer shawl!

NEIL. Yes! The prayer shawl which is called the...

CINDY. Tallis!

> *(**NEIL** holds up more cards in rapid succession.)*

NEIL.
    HALACHA!

CINDY.
    JEWISH LAW!

NEIL.
    HAGGADAH!

CINDY.
    PURIM?

NEIL.
    NAH!

> *(Gives hints.)*

    FROGS! BLOOD! PLAGUES! MATZOH!

CINDY.
    PASSOVER...?

NEIL.
    TA-DAH!

BOTH.
    FAMILY FLASHCARDS!
    HOW HIGH CAN YOU SCORE

NEIL.
    FROM THE YEAR OF THE BOAR

CINDY.
> TO THE BLESSING FOR THE TORAH READING!

BOTH.
> FAMILY TENSIONS
> GET WAY OUT OF HAND
> 'LESS YOU LEARN TO SAY THE BRU-CHA
> THE MESHPUCHA DEMAND!

NEIL. Ganbei!

CINDY. Mazel tov! And now I believe it's *your* turn.

NEIL. Bring it on, baby!

> *(He concentrates. She shows him a card.)*

> "Ba jiao ho"...Shit, I know this...

CINDY. Tick, tick, tick, tick –

NEIL. The Tray of Togetherness! Different kinds of New Year's candies in a festive tray!

> *(**CINDY** nods, show him a new card.)*

> "Weilu." Too easy. The family banquet served on New Year's Eve.

CINDY. "Too easy," says the round eye.

NEIL. *(As she sorts through her cards.)* Let's face it. Jews know everything. We read, we study –

CINDY. Oh, really?

> *(She snaps out a card.)*

> HUANG DOU JIANG!

NEIL. *(Spoken in rhythm.)*
> FISH SAUCE?

CINDY. *(Makes buzzer sound for wrong answer.)*
> SOY.

(She pulls out the next card.)

CINDY.

MAN-MAN-CHI!

NEIL. *(Spoken.)*

RELAX?

CINDY. *(Spoken in ryhthm.)*

ENJOY.

*(She shakes **NEIL**'s hand.)*

(Sung.)

GUONIAN!

NEIL.

BAINIAN!

CINDY. *(She pulls out the next card.)*

CÈSUÔ ZÀI NÂLI?

NEIL.

THAT MEANS...WHERE'S THE JOHN!

CINDY. Good boy!

BOTH.

FAMILY FLASHCARDS!

YA' GOTTA PREPARE –

NEIL.

OR TIANNEMEN SQUARE

MAY DESTABILIZE THE PEACE PROCEEDING.

CINDY.

CULTURAL CARNAGE

YA' WANNA AVOID –

BOTH.

KID, YA' BETTER GET YOUR MISSILES

OF CONTAINMENT DEPLOYED!

CINDY. Lights out! That was good.

NEIL. Not good enough. Time for the lightning round.

CINDY. The lightning round?

NEIL. No hints, no hesitation, eye of the tiger. Ready?

CINDY. Ready –

*(**NEIL** flashes a card.)*

"Bimah." That platform thing where they hold the Torah service.

(He nods. She flashes a card.)

NEIL. "Zaowang." Kitchen God, guardian of the hearth, big deal on New Year's Day.

(She nods. He flashes a card.)

CINDY. "Chuppah." The wedding tent, the canopy.

(He nods. She flashes a card; the pace is picking up.)

NEIL. "Yuan Hsiao Jie!" The New Year's Festival of Lanterns!

(He flashes a card.)

CINDY. "Kiddush!" The blessing of the wine before the meal!

(Snap! She flashes another card.)

NEIL. "Gong Xi Fa Tsai Xin Nian Kuai Le!" Good luck!

CINDY. Right.

(Snap! He flashes a final card.)

"Sandy Koufax!"...Sandy Koufax?

NEIL. No hints! No hesitation!

CINDY. He was a baseball player. What's that got to do with –

NEIL. Here comes the buzzer!

CINDY. Wait, are you saying he was *Jewish*?

NEIL. *(Makes a sound like a buzzer.)* That's it! She got 'em all! Bring on the Mandelbaums!

CINDY. Next stop the Ch'en Family banquet!

> *(More flashcards, coming fast and furious.)*

NEIL.
MILKEDICH?

CINDY.
DAIRY FOOD!

NEIL.
MIKVAH!

CINDY.
BATH!

> *(Her turn.)*

> *(Spoken in rhythm.)*

CHICKEN?

NEIL.
JI! *(Pronounced "gee".)*

CINDY.
OOLONG?

NEIL.
TEA!

> *(His turn.)*

HITLER!

CINDY.
PSYCHOPATH!

NEIL. *(Sung.)*
PORK!

CINDY.
TRAFE!

NEIL. *(Spoken in rhythm.)*
PARVE!

CINDY.
SAFE!

NEIL. *(Sung.)*
MO-TZE!

CINDY.
LECH-EM!

NEIL.
BO-RAY!

CINDY.
PREE!
WEN AN!

NEIL.
ZAI JIAN!

CINDY. *(Spoken in rhythm.)*
BINGO!

NEIL.
MAH-JONG!

BOTH. *(Sung.)*
ALLY-ALLY-OXEN-FREE!
FAMILY FLASHCARDS!
YOU GOTTA GET RIGHT,
OR THE FAMILIES FIGHT
ON THE GENOCIDE OF INTER-BREEDING.
HAPPILY AFTER
GETS TOTALLY SCREWED
IF YOU LOUSE IT UP AND CAUSE AN INTER-FAMILY FEUD!
FAMILY FLASHCARDS,
A YUK AND A HALF!

CINDY.

THOUGH THE FAMILIES ARE FURIOUS,

NEIL.

DECLARE THE UNION SPURIOUS,

BOTH.

THE DAMAGE AIN'T INJURIOUS

(They kiss.)

JUST AS LONG AS YA' LAUGH!

(They do, with the promise of something steamy to follow, as the subway doors slide closed and they disappear. MIGUEL grins.)

MIGUEL. My man, Neil. Who knew he had it in him?

ZACK. When I was growing up in Grand Rapids I had a friend named Neil. Nervous. Jewish. I had dinner at his house one night. The food was weird. Fish chopped up and turned into fish. But what really spooked me was the *noise*. Because at my house dinner was like a picnic in a mausoleum. Total silence. Except, of course, for my father. Who saw an intimate meal with his only son as a golden opportunity to kick some cross-examination ass. Fourth grade. I'm studying South America. I've got my soup spoon half way to my mouth when, bang: What's the capitol of Ecuador? What's the highest mountain in the Andes? Name five tributaries of the Orinoco. And you know the weirdest part? I thought this was all entirely normal. He was a lawyer. His father was a lawyer. His *brother* was a lawyer. So I just figured, I wanted to be a lawyer, too. It's like I stepped on this moving sidewalk that went through Andover and Dartmouth and Harvard Law School. And I never once stepped off. Until I found myself on this subway car, it never even *occurred* to me to step off.

GINA. When's the last time you saw your father?

ZACK. I haven't been home since I finished law school.

MIGUEL. Kids gotta see their dads, man.

STANLEY. But given your current circumstances, I don't think you'll be seeing yours anytime soon –

ARLENE. *(Cutting him off.)* Oh, why don't you cut the kid some slack? It's not like he *chose* to take a ride on your weird post-mortem choo-choo.

STANLEY. Funny, I thought that's exactly what he did.

ARLENE. Fine. What if he did? People make choices all the time. Good ones. Bad ones. He did. I did. It wouldn't kill you to show a little –

STANLEY. Empathy?

ARLENE. Yes. Empathy.

STANLEY. Wait a minute! What happened to that whole "making moral judgments isn't racquetball" thing?

ARLENE. Come on my program, asshole. We'll discuss it.

STANLEY. You know I'd love to, Arlene, except you don't have a program. And, just for the record, I don't see you getting any closer to choosing your moment.

MIGUEL. Excuse me, if it's cool with everybody, I actually think *I'm* ready to pick.

ARLENE. *Whoa*! "Cool" with everybody? Not with everybody. I didn't get killed by a peach pit so I could watch you get a blow job in a broom closet –

*(To **GINA**, indicating her iPod and headphones.)*

You mind if I borrow those?

MIGUEL. It's funny. I'm a little bit embarrassed.

ARLENE. *(As she puts the headphones on.)* Impossible.

MIGUEL. *(To* STANLEY.*)* This always works? I'm not gonna end up like, at the opera or in Iraq, right?

(Lights come up on…)

[MUSIC NO. 10A - "KNOCK KNOCK"]

Yolanda's Bedroom

(**MIGUEL***'s no-nonsense ex-wife,* **JUANITA***, enters with a laundry basket. Her eight-year-old daughter,* **YOLANDA***, sits on her bed, showing a tooth to her friend* **VICTOR***.*)

JUANITA.   Yolanda, it's eight o'clock. You got your homework done, right?

YOLANDA.   Yes, Mami.

JUANITA.   Victor. Your Mami just called. She wants you home half an hour ago.

YOLANDA.   I was just showing Victor my tooth.

VICTOR.   Whoa!

JUANITA.   So now Victor has seen the famous tooth and we can all say *Buenas noches* to Victor.

YOLANDA.   See you in school, Victor!

(**VICTOR** *exits.* **YOLANDA** *watches* **JUANITA** *as she folds laundry.*)

You know, last week Millie lost a tooth and the Tooth Fairy left her a dollar. And the week before Jorge got *two* dollars!

JUANITA.   Which is very nice for Jorge and Millie. But you and me, baby, we live in a different world. We live in a real world, where I have to work three jobs to make up for your deadbeat Papi who never makes his child support payments on time and who thinks that a good job for a thirty-two year old man is riding a bicycle around the Bronx. So instead of putting that tooth under your pillow, we are going to put it here –

(*She takes the tooth and drops it in the waste basket.* **YOLANDA** *looks crestfallen.*)

JUANITA. Because there is no make-believe fairy going to come in here and turn it into money, you understand?

YOLANDA. Yes, Mami.

JUANITA. Now, time for bed. You got school tomorrow.

> (**JUANITA** *tucks* **YOLANDA** *in, kisses her on the forehead, turns out the light, and leaves.*)
>
> (*A beat, then* **YOLANDA** *rolls over, roots around in the waste basket, finds the tooth and puts it under her pillow.*)
>
> (*Before she can get back into bed, a crash from the fire escape. The subway doors slide open as* **MIGUEL** *tumbles through the bedroom window.*)

YOLANDA. Who's that?! Who's there?! I got a gun!

> (**MIGUEL** *pops up, hands in the air. He is wearing an odd, improvised, Tooth Fairy-like costume.*)

MIGUEL. Wait, wait, wait –!

YOLANDA. The Tooth Fairy! I knew you'd come!

MIGUEL. *(Instantly relaxing, snapping back into character.)* Hey, whenever a sweet little cuchifrito like you loses a tooth the Tooth Fairy *always* comes! Who told you the Tooth Fairy wasn't coming?

YOLANDA. My Mami. She said we lived in a real world with deadbeat Papis and Mamis who had to work three jobs and in the real world there was no Tooth Fairy.

MIGUEL. She told you that, huh? Well, the Tooth Fairy's heard that kind of jive before, kid. In fact, he heard it in a lawyer's office just yesterday afternoon. And your Mami isn't wrong. The real world is one helluva tough place. But that's how come you gotta never stop believing that cool, crazy, magical things can happen in that world. They can happen to you, and you can *make* them happen, you got it?

(**YOLANDA** *nods.*)

MIGUEL. O.K., now let's do some business. You got the tooth?

(**YOLANDA** *takes it out from under her pillow, hands it to* **MIGUEL.***)*

[MUSIC NO. 11 "THE TOOTH FAIRY SONG"]

Whoa! This is one diente excelente! So the Tooth Fairy gets this excellent tooth and the little girl gets an excellent reward for being so brave.

SING!

SING THE TOOTH FAIRY SONG!

YOLANDA. *(Spoken in rhythm.)*
WHAT 'TOOTH FAIRY SONG?'

MIGUEL. *(As if everybody's heard of it.)*
THE TOOTH FAIRY SONG!
MAKE THE MAGIC WORDS UP AS YOU GO ALONG...
WHEN YOU SING
THE TOOTH FAIRY SONG!

YOLANDA.
I'M SINGING THE SONG,
THE TOOTH FAIRY SONG.

MIGUEL.
NOW DANCE THE TOOTH FAIRY DANCE
AS GLITTERY MOONBEAMS
FLICKER AND PRANCE!
SPRINKLE FAIRY DUST ON YOUR PAJAMA PANTS...!
WHEN YOU DO
THE TOOTH FAIRY DANCE!

YOLANDA. *Whee!*

MIGUEL.
AND WE CAN FLY –!

YOLANDA.
WE CAN FLY –!

MIGUEL.
THROUGH STARRY NIGHTS –!

YOLANDA.
THROUGH STARRY NIGHTS –

MIGUEL.	**YOLANDA.**
IN THE SPELL	AH.
OF ENCHANTED VISITATION RIGHTS.	AH.

(He finds a pinwheel on the window sill.)

I WAVE MY WAND –!
YOU SHUT YOUR EYES –!
AND ABRACADABARA
COMES A BRAVE GIRL'S PRIZE!

Two big, beautiful, bright shiny quarters –

(He pulls them magically out of her ears.)

Sweet, huh?

YOLANDA. It's a dollar.

MIGUEL. What's a dollar?

YOLANDA. For the tooth. Millie got a dollar. Jorge got *two* dollars –

MIGUEL. O.K., O.K., Jesus...

(He digs around in his pockets, finds nothing.)

MIGUEL. You know, it looks like the Tooth Fairy left his wallet in his other tutu. But I got another idea. I knew a little girl once, she was a lot like you...

(He reaches under the bed, takes out a cigar box which **YOLANDA** *has decorated with pictures cut out of magazines, snapshots of her family, etc.)*

...and she kept all her treasures in a pretty little box under –

YOLANDA. *(Snatching a purse from out of the box.)* You want me to *lend* you the money?

MIGUEL. Hey, let's not get all snotty with the Tooth Fairy, huh?

YOLANDA. Whatever...

(She takes a dollar out of the box, and hands it to him.)

Here.

MIGUEL. And here, Princess...

(He makes the dollar disappear –.)

YOLANDA. Hey!

MIGUEL. (*–As he magically reveals it underneath her pillow.)*...is your dollar.

YOLANDA. Whoa! Thanks, Tooth Fairy!

MIGUEL.
NOW SHAKE THE TOOTH FAIRY TUSH.

YOLANDA.
AND LOOKIT YOUR TUTU SHIMMY AND SWOOSH –

MIGUEL.
TWIRLING WITH A WHIRLING BALLERINA WHOOSH –

BOTH. *(As they dance.)*
AS YOU SHAKE THE TOOTH FAIRY TUSH

MIGUEL. *Whoa!*
> WE GOT THE MOVES –!
> TO BEAT THE BAND –!
> THE BRONX
> MAKES THE CHILI CLUB LOOK LIKE DISNEYLAND.

YOLANDA. Disneyland! You promised to take me to Disneyland!

> *(A knock on the door.)*

JUANITA. *(Offstage.)* Yolanda, what's going on in there?

YOLANDA. Nothing, Mami!

MIGUEL. Time for the Tooth Fairy to move on to the next little cuchifrito who lost a tooth, O.K., baby?

YOLANDA. O.K., Tooth Fairy.

> *(**MIGUEL** tucks **YOLANDA** into bed.)*

MIGUEL. *(More tenderly.)*
> NOW DREAM THE TOOTH FAIRY DREAM
> OF PEARLY WHITE TEETH
> THAT DAZZLE AND GLEAM.
> SMILE AND YOU'LL SURPRISE YOURSELF
> HOW BRIGHT THINGS SEEM.

YOLANDA. *(As he starts to climb out the window.)* Papi, don't go!

MIGUEL. I got to, baby. But here –

> *(He hands her the pinwheel.)*

When I'm gone, you blow on this pinwheel and think of me and the wheels of my bike spinning with cool, crazy, magical love for you.

YOLANDA. I love you, Papi.

MIGUEL. Not half as much as I love you, Princess.

(He sends her a kiss.)

BABY, DREAM –

(She blows on the pinwheel and jumps in his arms.)

BOTH.
THE TOOTH FAIRY DREAM.

(The subway doors slide closed and **MIGUEL** *and* **YOLANDA** *disappear...)*

GINA. Can you imagine if you had a little girl like that...?

ARLENE. He didn't have to imagine. She was real and he hardly ever saw her.

ZACK. Maybe. But he's seeing her now.

ARLENE. Is he? All these "happy moments," no matter what kind of life you led. Aren't people supposed to get what they *deserve*?

STANLEY. And what do you think you deserve, Arlene?

ARLENE. *(Shrugs, holds up her tote.)* I was in Bergdorf's one afternoon. I saw this bag. *Ferragamo.* Twelve hundred bucks. I couldn't decide if I wanted the navy or the beige so I got one of each. Maybe that should be my perfect moment.

ZACK. I think you can come up with a better moment than that, Arlene.

STANLEY. Here's an idea. How 'bout the Kennedy Assassination?

ARLENE. Shut up! You soulless little fascist twit! I handed out leaflets for John F. Kennedy! Bobby Kennedy was my Senator! I organized the Mount Holyoke campus for Gene McCarthy, and the night of the New Hampshire primary when McCarthy gave Lyndon Johnson his first big shove out of the White House, that was one of the greatest moments of my life!

ZACK. Am I hearing this? Is everybody hearing this?

ARLENE. "Hey, hey, LBJ. How many kids did you kill today?!" We beat that. At least for that one night, we beat that.

ZACK. And then what happened to you? Jesus Christ, Arlene, what happened?

ARLENE. What happened? McCarthy got creamed, Bobby got shot, Nixon got elected. The Sixties were finished. We didn't want to wind up in the gutter, toothless and irrelevant, with nothing but a set of love beads and a bong. So we all got jobs – on Wall Street, in broadcasting. We told ourselves we were growing up... but what we were really doing was selling out. We lost our voice. I broke the faith. I want it back. I want to fix it. *(Guitar lick.)*

March 12, 1968? Me and the other Peaceniks were down in Union Square watching the returns coming in from New Hampshire... McCarthy hit forty percent...we just went crazy...someone said, "We gotta go celebrate!" ...and back then there was only one place to go...

ANNOUNCER. *(Offstage.)* Ladies and Gentlemen, The Fillmore East is proud to present...*Spooky Tooth*!

[MUSIC NO. 12 "THE ROAD TO NIRVANA"]

(The subway doors open on a psychedelic vision of...)

The Fillmore East Stage

(...Where Spooky Tooth is rocking out with electric basses, guitars, moog synthesizer, and sitars. Ceiling lights zig-zag back and forth over the bobbing Fillmore **CROWD**. **ARLENE** *walks through the subway doors and disappears into the* **CROWD**.*)*

LUTHER. Rock 'n' Roll, New York! Are you ready for it?!... I can't hear you...!

> *(***ARLENE** *reappears, transformed, wearing bell bottoms and a tie-dyed blouse.)*

ARLENE.
AT THE HEIGHT OF THE SIXTIES
EMPOWERED BY YOUTH,
WE WERE ROCKIN' THE SYSTEM!
WE WERE FIGHTING FOR TRUTH!
SO WE ALL CROWDED INTO
MY DODGE CORONET
TO THE FILLMORE TO MOVE
WHERE THE GROOVY-DOOVY LET IT HANG OUT!
TRIPPIN' ON ACID,
PEYOTE AND 'SHROOMS,
PSYCHEDELICALLY FLYIN'
IN FRANKINCENSE FUMES
IT WAS SPOOKY TOOTH PLAYIN'
THE NUMBER ONE SONG,
ME AND TWO-THOUSAND STONERS
ALL BOBBIN' ALONG, SINGIN'...

> *(Focus shifts to* **LUTHER**, *the lead singer for Spooky Tooth, up onstage, and the Fillmore* **CROWD** *bobbing below him.* **ARLENE** *gets lost in the* **CROWD** *again.)*

LUTHER.
SHOW ME THE ROAD TO NIRVANA!

CROWD.
SHA-NANA, SHANA-NANA!

LUTHER.
SHOW ME THE ROAD TO NIRVANA!

CROWD.
SHA-NANA-NANA!

> (**ARLENE** *reappears in a wig of long, hippie hair.*)

ARLENE.	**CROWD.**
IN MY TIE-DYES AND BELLS,	OOH.
HIPPIE NECKLACE OF SHELLS,	OOH.
AND MICHELLE PHILLIPS HAIR	
WITH MY WOUNDED-KNEE BANDANA, IT WAS –	
SHOW ME THE ROAD TO NIRVANA!	

CROWD.
SHA-NANA, SHANA-NANA!

LUTHER & ARLENE.
SHOW ME THE ROAD TO NIRVANA!

CROWD.
SHA-NANA-NANA!

LUTHER. *(Spoken in rhythm.)*
YOU AN' ME GROOVY GIRL,
WE CAN CHANGE THIS WHOLE WORL'

LUTHER, ARLENE & CROWD.
HEADIN' HIGH'R AN' HIGH'R
DOWN A HIGHWAY OF FIRE
IN A RAINBOW OF HEAVENLY

LUTHER & ARLENE.
MANNA!

CROWD.
SHA-NANA, SHANA-NANA!

LUTHER, ARLENE & CROWD.
SHOW ME THE ROAD TO NIRVANA!

LUTHER. *(A deafening rock 'n' roll scream.)*
YAAAAAAAH!!!

> (**ARLENE** *cringes and marches back into the subway car.*)

ZACK. Jesus, she's coming back!

GINA. Can she come back like that?

STANLEY. We've got rules here, Arlene. Is this your moment or not?

ARLENE. I don't know. I'm conflicted.

ZACK. *Conflicted?*

ARLENE. It's a big commitment, eternity. There's a few things about that night I forgot to remember. Like Jason Fitterman –

> *(Lights up on...)*

The Fillmore, Backstage

> (*...Where* **JASON** *is aggressively feeling up a girl named* **GINNY**.)

JASON. Mmmm, baby. Oh, baby.

GINNY. Mmmm. Ohhh.

ARLENE. He was my boyfriend.

Look at him, that son of a bitch...and she wasn't even pretty. She had a moustache.

> (**ARLENE** *marches back through the subway doors.*)

GINA. You go, girl!

ARLENE.
THERE WAS JASON WITH GINNY
FROM GET-OUT-THE-VOTE,
WITH HIS HAND INSIDE HER MINI
AND HIS TONGUE DOWN HER THROAT.

> (**ARLENE** *swats* **JASON**.)

JASON. *(Spoken in rhythm.)*
I'M A DUDE, SHE'S A CHICK,
SO BE COOL, BABY, CHILL.

ARLENE. *(Spoken in rhythm.)*
WHO'S NOT "COOL"? I'M NOT "COOL"?

> *(Sung.)*
WELL, GO DROOL ON MISS DEPILATORY!

> *(She bolts for a backstage bathroom, where the door to one of the stalls is beginning to open...)*

ARLENE.

RAN TO THE BATHROOM
TO CRY OUT MY EYES,
WHEN THE DOOR TO THE THIRD STALL
OPENS UP AND *SURPRISE:*
WHO COMES SAUNTERING OUT
AS HE BUTTONS HIS FLY?
IT WAS MICK! JAGGER, MICK!
CROSS MY HEART SWEAR TA' DIE!

MICK. Hi.

> (**MICK** *gives* **ARLENE** *the pouty lips and an extremely meaningful look.*)

LUTHER.

SHOW ME THE ROAD TO NIRVANA!

MICK. *(Spoken in rhythm.)*
SHA-NANA?

ARLENE. *(Spoken in rhythm.)*
NANA-NANA...

LUTHER.

SHOW ME THE ROAD TO NIRVANA!

MICK. *(Spoken in rhythm.)*
SHA-NANA?

ARLENE. *(A shrug to* **MICK,** *why not?)*

> *(Spoken in rhythm.)*

NANA.

> *(Sung.)*

WHEN HE GAVE ME THOSE LIPS,
DID THAT THING WITH HIS HIPS,
I WAS DAMNED IF I'D WAIT FOR MAÑANA.

CROWD.
SHA-NA-NA, SHANA-NANA!

MICK, ARLENE & CROWD.
SHOW ME THE ROAD TO NIRVANA.

> *(**ARLENE** follows **MICK** into the bathroom stall, disappears for a moment, then reappears and scurries back toward the subway car.)*

MICK. Baby, baby, don't leave me hanging.

GINA. Arlene?

STANLEY. Again?

ARLENE. *(To **STANLEY**.)* O.K., mark it down. This is it.

> *(To **GINA**.)*

Gloss.

> *(**GINA** hands her lip gloss from her purse.)*

ZACK. Wait a minute. You mean *that's* your moment? After all the grief you gave Miguel? Arlene Slater's perfect moment is a "happy ending" she gave Mick Jagger backstage at the Fillmore East?!

ARLENE. No, no, no. The moment wasn't just about sex. It was about levitating the Pentagon, raising our voices, and changing the world.

> *(To **GINA** as she heads back out into the Fillmore.)*

But you know that lyric? "I can't get no satisfaction." Not true. Not even close.

> *(**ARLENE** walks back through the subway doors to **MICK**. The people in the **CROWD** light lighters and hold them aloft.)*

ARELENE.	CROWD.
WE *BOTH* HAD A...	AH!
HAPPY ENDING.	HAPPY ENDING. AH!
A TANTRIC REVELATION	AH! AH! AH!
AND WITH NO HESITATION,	AH! AH!!
WE'LL COME ONCE MORE,	WE WILL COME ONCE MORE!
'CAUSE *I'LL* HAVE A	
HAPPY ENDING,	HAPPY ENDING,
INSIDE THESE FILLMORE HALLWAYS,	INSIDE THESE FILLMORE HALLWAYS,
AND BE THE ME I ALWAYS WAS BEFORE...	AH...

> (**MICK** *struts around the stage, while the hippies adorn* **ARLENE** *with flowers, beads, and a peace symbol necklace.*)

ARLENE & CROWD.
BACK TO HENDRIX AND CREAM,
THE SUPREMES AND DIANA,

ARLENE.
NO REAGAN, NO BUSH,
MTV OR MADONNA...
...BACK TO A ME I LIKED BETTTER!

LUTHER & CROWD.
SHA-NANA, SHANA-NANA!

ARLENE.
MINUS THE PUMPS, PEARLS AND SWEATER!

LUTHER & CROWD.
SHA-NANA-NANA!

ARLENE.	CROWD.
WITH A KARMIC EMBRACE	OOH!
FOR THE WHOLE HUMAN RACE,	FOR THE WHOLE HUMAN RACE
HEADIN'...	HEADIN'...

ARLENE, MICK & CROWD.
HIGH'R AN' HIGH'R
DOWN A HIGHWAY OF FIRE
IN A RAINBOW OF HEAVENLY MANNA!

CROWD.
SHA-NANA, SHANA-NANA!

ARLENE, MICK, LUTHER & CROWD.
BACK ON THE ROAD TO NIRVANA!

> (**MICK** *and* **ARLENE** *are embraced by the* **CROWD** *as the subway doors close on the Fillmore.*)

CROWD.
AH!

ZACK. I gotta hand it to her. That was not a moment I expected.

GINA. She picked great. And not just her. Miguel, Maurice...

STANLEY. There's a lot of different ways to choose. Some people are looking for redemption, others go for affirmation, and now we know some go directly for Mick Jagger.

> (**STANLEY** *performs one of Mick Jagger's moves.*)

ZACK. That's good. You look like Miguel's chicken.

STANLEY. Hey, I partied with Mick Jagger downstairs at Studio 54.

ZACK. Something to be really proud of –

GINA. *(Cutting them off.)* Stop it! Both of you! Everybody's picked but me and I can't choose! I don't know how! I've been living inside of this fantasy for so long I can't even *think* about choosing. I need help!

ZACK & STANLEY. Gina, listen –

(**STANLEY** *takes a step towards her, but* **ZACK** *steps in front of him.* **STANLEY** *takes a step back and watches.*)

ZACK. There's a life you lived, a real life, before you started to live the life you made up. I understand that. Moonlight doesn't just shine on the Matterhorn. There must have been moonlight back in that real life.

GINA. Back in Brooklyn? It's not Gstaad.

ZACK. That's where you're from? From Brooklyn?

GINA. (*A sudden chip on her shoulder.*) Hey, Jerry Seinfeld's from Brooklyn. So's Tony Danza, and Walt Whitman –

ZACK. Gina, I'm fine with Brooklyn. *Peter Luger* is in Brooklyn.

GINA. *Peter Luger.* That was the family business, restaurants. Well, no, not restaurants. Pizza joints. We owned a couple of 'em. *The Napoli* and *The Sorrento.* That's where I worked. After school. Summer vacations. That was my life before I moved to Manhattan.

ZACK. So I guess you weren't drinking a lot of chilled *Cristal* back then.

GINA. Malt liquor in twenty-two ounce cans.

ZACK. Not a bad drink on a hot summer night. What else? Think back, Gina. What do you see?

GINA. Just Brooklyn. The Verrazano Narrows Bridge. Marie's Bridal. Faicco's Pork Store...

(*A beat. She smiles.*)

ZACK. What?

GINA. Faicco's. They had this pig out front with a saddle on its back. One of those twenty-five cent rides for little kids. When we dumped our boyfriends we'd write their names in magic marker on the pig's ass.

ZACK. I'll bet you did a lot of writing...

GINA. *(Another smile.)* Boyfriends...

ZACK. And this was where exactly?

[MUSIC NO. 13 "GSTAAD (REPRISE)"]

GINA.
> BAY RIDGE.

ZACK. Bay Ridge?

GINA.
> I SEE BAY RIDGE.
> BUSSING TABLES AT THE FAM'LY PIZZERIA.
> WITH THIS CUTE ITALIAN GUY
> WHO'D BEEN GIVIN' ME THE EYE.
> MARCELLO FROM COSENZA, CALABRIA.

> *(The subway doors open. There he is,*
> **MARCELLO**, *leaning on the railing on...)*

The Boardwalk at Coney Island

(...Staring out at the moonlit sea.)

MARCELLO. Gina.

> (**GINA** *looks at* **ZACK**, *who smiles, then very tentatively she walks through the doors, joining* **MARCELLO**...)

GINA.
ONE SUMMER NIGHT,
WE GOT ONTO THE TRAIN,
AND RODE TO CONEY ISLAND, THE BOARDWALK.
AND AS THE MOON ROSE OVER THE FERRIS WHEEL,
IT WAS LIKE THE PARIS TUILERIES...
EXCEPT THAT IT WAS REAL.
THE SAND, SO CLEAN AND WHITE.
NOT A CONDOM OR A PEPSI CAN IN SIGHT.

> (**MARCELLO**, *trying one of the boardwalk games, tosses a bean bag and wins a stuffed bear, which he hands to her proudly.)*

AND WHEN HE WON A CARE BEAR
IN PURPLE PLUSH,
WELL, I SWORE, THIS WAS MORE THAN A CRUSH.

> (**MARCELLO** *picks* **GINA** *up and sets her down on the subway car, now magically transformed into a carousel, on which she dances. She grabs the brass ring.)*

MARCELLO. Va bene, Gina!...Che bellezza!...La mia stella!
...Mio amore!

> *(He lifts her off the car.)*

GINA. *(Beaming at the Care Bear.)* Marcello, it's *sooooo cu-ute.* And purple is the only color that I didn't have!

MARCELLO. Penso ti amo, donna bella.

GINA. Whoa, cool it, paisano. You ever heard of *Vogue Magazine* in Calabria? Christie Brinkley modeling bathing suits in Majorca? Well, someday I'm gonna be her, so let's not get carried away here, O.K.? I'm not some Bay Ridge slut, like my cousin Adrianna.

MARCELLO. Sei molto più bella di Christie Brinkley.

GINA. Prettier than Christie? Cut it out…

MARCELLO. *(Inviting her to sit beside him on the sand.)* Siediti vicino a me sulla sabbia.

GINA.	MARCELLO.
WELL…OKAY.	PENSO TI AMO
I MEAN, FOR NOW.	BELLA DONNA.
COUSIN ADRIANNA'S	STRINGI
GONNA HAVE A COW…	LA MIA MANO.
IF SHE COULD SEE THIS	QUANTO BELLA…
MOONLIGHT,	
THIS PERFECT SCENE	COSI BELLA…
LIKE A PAGE	
OUT OF VOGUE	
MAGAZINE…	

>   *(GINA lets her head fall on MARCELLO's lap, gazes at the stars and the ocean.)*

ZACK. Gina.

>   *(GINA turns, looks at ZACK, as if she were in both the past and the present at the same time.)*

GINA.
SO SERENE, SO SUBLIME…
AND WHO KNEW IT WAS HERE,
RIGHT HERE,
OH SO NEAR
ALL THE TIME.

*(**MARCELLO** takes **GINA**'s hand as the subway doors slide closed and they disappear... **ZACK** looks down and discovers – the purple care bear.)*

ZACK. Look at this.

STANLEY. Read what it says on the label.

ZACK. "Made in the People's Republic of China."

STANLEY. *(Cutting him off.)* Other side.

ZACK. "To Zack. Be happy, and thanks." Signed Gina, with a smiley-face. How...?

STANLEY. Don't ask me to explain the metaphysics. I just work here –

(A beat.)

Listen, I lost it a little bit back there. With them. With you. I don't do that.

ZACK. You had a bad day.

STANLEY. You did good.

*(**ZACK** nods.)*

ZACK. I gotta go back, Stanley.

STANLEY. Zack, I *told* you –

ZACK. I know what you told me. But I'm a different person. I'm *becoming* a different person, I can feel it! Gimme a second chance!

STANLEY. A second chance. Like you're the only one who'd like a second chance.

ZACK. I know, I understand. But you died, I didn't. You can't *change* the moments in your life. *I can.* Dozens of moments, *thousands* of moments! All completely different from the life I lead before! Please, Stanley! Help me!

STANLEY. Zack, *I can't.* If I could open up those doors, I would, but I don't have that power –

[MUSIC NO. 14 "HAPPINESS"]

ZACK. *(Cutting him off.)*
DON'T TELL ME YOUR HANDS ARE TIED.

STANLEY. *Zack* –

ZACK.
DON'T BRUSH ME THE HELL ASIDE.
I'M PLEADING, WITHOUT AN OUNCE OF PRIDE...

STANLEY. No pleading, please. It's creepy –

ZACK.
GIVE ME A CHANCE TO LAY CLAIM
TO THE NAME OF THE COMEBACK KID.
HERE I HAVE SEEN, WELL, I MEAN
I DESERVE A GREEN LIGHT.
NAME ME A LESSON, I'VE LEARNED IT.
I'VE EARNED IT, YOU *KNOW* I DID:
HAPPINESS, MY CHANCE TO MAKE THINGS RIGHT.

STANLEY. I understand, Zack, but –

ZACK.
NOT ON YOUR LIST, NOT A CHANCE
I'D BE MISSED IF YOU SET ME FREE.
BACK ON THE STREET,
ONLY NOW WITH MY FEET ON THE GROUND.
GIVE ME MY SHOT, THE ONE YOU
NEVER GOT, YOU CAN GIVE TO ME:
HAPPINESS, THE SECOND TIME AROUND.

STANLEY. Zack, I can't *do* it.

ZACK.
A SECOND CHANCE
TO BE A BRAVER MAN,

ZACK.
> AND TURN MY "NO YOU CAN'TS"
> AROUND TO "YES I CAN."
> TO SEIZE EVERY DAY
> AS LONG AS I LIVE,
> AND KNOW THAT THE GREATEST JOY
> I WILL EVER HAVE IS THE JOY I GIVE.

STANLEY. There are no second acts in American lives, Zack.

ZACK. *Says who?*

STANLEY. F. Scott Fitzgerald.

ZACK. Fuck F. Scott Fitzgerald! I'm asking *you*, Stanley!

ZACK.
> PRESS ME A BUTTON AND
> OPEN
> SOME MAGICAL SAFETY
> HATCH!

STANLEY.
> THERE'S NO SUCH
> BUTTON.

ZACK.
> GIVE ME THE PIN
> TO THE SECRET SECURITY
> CARD!

STANLEY.
> YOU'RE STUCK HERE,
> SAME AS I.

ZACK.	**STANLEY.**
FIND ME A LOOPHOLE,	
A LEVER UNLOCKING	NO LOOPHOLE.
THE EXIT LATCH,	ZACK,
AND LET ME GO!	IT ISN'T ANY USE.
IS THAT SO HARD?	AND THAT'S SO HARD.

STANLEY. It doesn't have to be that bad, Zack. O.K., you're going to ride some train alone forever. But I had a Buddhist Monk come through here who would have killed for that chance. And if you think of all the total schmucks you'll never have to deal with again, being alone won't seem so bad –

ZACK. *No*!

I WANT WHAT'S FAIR!
I DON'T BELONG IN HERE!
I BELONG OUT THERE!
SO HEAR ME LOUD AND CLEAR!
SOME NATURAL LAWS
HAVE GOT TO APPLY!
FOR TOO MANY YEARS I'VE LIVED
WITH MY HEART ON PAUSE.
JUST ONCE BEFORE I DIE...
I WANNA...
...DANCE IN THE ARMS OF A GIRL
I ADORE, AND THEN LEARN HER NAME!
TALK ABOUT SPORTS WITH MY DAD,
AND BE THERE FOR A FRIEND!
DO CONEY ISLAND
AND GO WITH MY SON TO A BASEBALL GAME!

STANLEY.

OR FALL IN LOVE –

ZACK.

AND HAVE A TRULY

ZACK & STANLEY.

"HAPPY ENDING"!

ZACK.

LOOK AT ME WORLD, WHO YOU SEE
IS A ME NO ONE'S EVER KNOWN!
I DON'T KNOW HOW BUT THE CHANGE
IN ME NOW IS PROFOUND!

SOMEWHERE BACK HOME IN NEW YORK
IS A MOMENT THAT'S ALL MY OWN!
ONE PERFECT ONE
THAT'S MINE ALONE!
NOT TOO LATE TO FIND IT, I'M
GONNA HAVE IT IN MY PRIME:

ZACK.

HAPPINESS!
HAPPINESS!
HAPPINESS
THE SECOND TIME AROUND!

*(Suddenly, magically – at the pinnacle of Zack's last note – the subway doors open. **ZACK** stares, astounded, then spins back to **STANLEY**, who looks equally astounded.)*

ZACK. You did it –

STANLEY. I didn't do anything. You. You did it.

*(Handing **ZACK** his briefcase.)*

Go on. Get out of here! Go! Go!

*(**ZACK** rushes through the doors, stops and looks back at **STANLEY** as he and the subway car disappear. In front of him, there is a –.)*

Turnstile

> (**ZACK** *races toward it, as the same attractive* **YOUNG WOMAN**, *carrying the same shopping bag from Whole Foods, enters.* **ZACK** *crashes into her. Clementines roll everywhere.*)

ZACK. Oh, shit. Hey, I'm sorry –

> (*He starts to bend down to pick them up.*)

YOUNG WOMAN. It's all right, I got it.

> (*A train horn sounds.*)

You're gonna miss your train.

ZACK. (*Collecting the last of the clementines.*) Don't worry about it...Here –

> (*Smiling, handing her the bag.*)

Here you go.

YOUNG WOMAN. Thanks.

> (*She smiles back and exits.*)

ZACK.
HERE'S A MOMENT I FIN'LLY NOTICE.
AWKWARD FEELINGS I CAN'T EXPLAIN...
SOMETIMES, MAYBE, IT'S GOOD TO MISS THE TRAIN.

> (*He notices one last errant clementine, scoops it up, and looks at it. He smiles, and follows the* **YOUNG WOMAN** *out of the station.*)

UNSEEN VOICES.
HAPPINESS!
HAPPINESS!
HAPPINESS!
HAPPINESS!

> (*Lights up on –.*)

The Interior of a Familiar Subway Car

(Half a dozen non descript **PASSENGERS** *sit here and there around the car.* **STANLEY** *appears, looking down at his clipboard –.)*

STANLEY. One, two, three, four, five, six –

(He counts the **PASSENGERS**.*)*

One, two, three, four, five, six. Thank God...

*(***STANLEY*** moves down to the pool of light which represents his trainman's compartment, speaking through his PA intercom.)*

Ladies and gentlemen, this is your trainman speaking –

(He dives into his familiar line of gibberish, but a lot has happened in the last hour and a half.)

O.K., listen up, everybody, the last group that came through here really took it outta me. Although they actually left me feeling pretty happy. Not happy enough to get me outta here, but that's another story. Anyway, give me a minute and I'll be out to get us started. In the meantime though, I'm going to save us both some time and trouble and cut right to the chase. You're all dead.

(He smiles, snaps off the intercom – starts to walk away and then turns back to the audience.)

BE HAPPY *NOW*, MY FRIENDS,
YOU KNOW THE WAY IT ENDS.
BLIPS...ON THE COSMIC RADAR.

*(***STANLEY*** steps into the car. The* **PASSENGERS** *scream.)*

(Blackout.)

[MUSIC NO. 16 "BOWS"]

[MUSIC NO. 17 "EXIT MUSIC"]

www.ingramcontent.com/pod-product-compliance
Lightning Source LLC
Chambersburg PA
CBHW070327120726
47909CB00008B/2624